"I Think We Have A Problem, Laura," Cabe Said.

Her brown eyes met his gaze squarely. "Not *we*, Cabe. I have no argument with what just happened," Laura replied, disconcertingly direct.

"All right, then, I have a problem."

"With what?"

"With you," he said chuckling. "I keep looking for a girl and finding a seductress in her place. You've grown into quite a woman, Laura. You set an ordinary man to shaking in his boots."

Laura felt a giddy taste of power. She brushed her knuckles across his mouth. "You're not an ordinary man, Cabe," she murmured.

"No, that I'm not. I'll have to stop forgetting that," he said, lowering his lips to capture hers in a kiss.

Dear Reader:

Series and Spin-offs! Connecting characters and intriguing interconnections to make your head whirl.

In Joan Hohl's successful trilogy for Silhouette Desire—*Texas Gold* (7/86), *California Copper* (10/86), *Nevada Silver* (1/87)—Joan created a cast of characters that just wouldn't quit. You figure out how *Lady Ice* (5/87) connects. And in August, "J.B." demanded his own story—*One Tough Hombre*. In *Falcon's Flight*, coming in November, you'll learn *all* about . . . ?

Annette Broadrick's *Return to Yesterday* (6/87) introduced Adam St. Clair. This August *Adam's Story* tells about the woman who saves his life—and teaches him a thing or two about love!

The six Branigan brothers appeared in Leslie Davis Guccione's *Bittersweet Harvest* (10/86) and *Still Waters* (5/87). September brings *Something in Common*, where the eldest of the strapping Irishmen finds love in unexpected places.

Midnight Rambler by Linda Barlow is in October—a special Halloween surprise, and totally unconnected to anything.

Keep an eye out for other Silhouette Desire favorites—Diana Palmer, Dixie Browning, Ann Major and Elizabeth Lowell, to name a few. You never know when secondary characters will insist on their own story. . . .

All the best,

Isabel Swift
Senior Editor & Editorial Coordinator
Silhouette Books

ASHLEY SUMMERS
Heart's Delight

Silhouette Desire

Published by Silhouette Books New York

America's Publisher of Contemporary Romance

SILHOUETTE BOOKS
300 East 42nd St., New York, N.Y. 10017

ISBN: 0-373-05374-6

First Silhouette Books printing September 1987

America's Publisher of Contemporary Romance

Printed in the U.S.A.

Books by Ashley Summers

Silhouette Romance

Season Enchantment #197
A Private Eden #223

Silhouette Desire

Fires of Memory #36
The Marrying Kind #95
Juliet #291
Heart's Delight #374

ASHLEY SUMMERS

is an incurable romantic who lives in Spring, Texas, in a ten-room house that overflows with family and friends. Her busy life revolves around the man she married thirty years ago, her three children, and handsome grandson, Eric. Formerly the owner and operator of a landscaping firm, she still enjoys maintaining her large yard and greenhouse. Other hobbies include biking, aerobics, reading and traveling.

One

The gray-green waters of the Cape Fear River stretched as far as the eye could see. Silhouetted against such immensity, the red and white speedboat straining at its tether assumed the fragility of a child's toy. With a thunderous roar, the motor came to life. The candy-cane craft left the pier at full throttle in a thrusting burst of power that pointed its sleek nose skyward for an instant. Just when it seemed on the verge of taking flight, the fiberglass hull touched water with the skimming motion of a dragonfly. Then it dipped to one side, turned in a dangerously tight arc and headed downstream.

The long, lean craft was decidedly masculine. Its driver was just as decidedly feminine. Masses of tawny brown curls lifted in the wind and floated out behind her like an exotic banner. The same wind molded her breasts against the fabric surely too fragile to contain their fullness. The man who watched her departure lowered his upraised arm and uttered a muffled oath. In his forest-green eyes a battle of ad-

miration and disbelief was fought. His face wore the slightly
stunned expression of a man whose over-confident stride
had just slammed him into a glass door.

Cabe McClain labeled himself three kinds of an idiot for
what a moment of indecision had cost him. He was supposed to meet her in town. Arriving early, he had driven instead to her house, hoping to catch her before she left to
keep their appointment, only to catch sight of her running
across the lawn to a small private dock.

But there had still been time enough, Cabe chided himself. Had he not paused to gawk like some moon-struck adolescent he could have stopped her. If he had not forgotten
how to speak, he could have called her name—but he wasn't
sure he *knew* her name. He was looking for Laura Richards. But that captivating creature bore scant resemblance
to the girl he remembered.

Little Mary Laura Richards. A smile softened the stern
cast of his features as her name whispered through his mind.
She had been been six years old the first time he saw her. All
knees and elbows, a funny little owl-eyed pixie who peered
out at the world from behind big, round glasses, her pipe-
stem form perennially clad in a pair of blue and white striped
overalls with patches on a bony little rump that begged to be
swatted.

She was thirteen and relatively unchanged when he left
town. She would be twenty-seven now. And watching the
tight, round bottom she'd swung across the yard... It wasn't
swatting that came to mind.

Chagrined by the eroticism tainting his thoughts, Cabe
raked his fingers through the dark, lustrous hair that swept
back in a widow's peak from his high brow. Of course it was
Laura driving that red and white speedboat. He had caught
only a brief glimpse of her face, but he'd know that pert
nose and stubborn point of chin anywhere—and what's with
you, McClain? he mocked the warmth swirling in his loins.
Both amused and disgusted at his reaction, he made his
careful way back to his car.

Self-annoyance thinned his full mouth as he added one more *if* to his aggravation list. If he had kept his wits and stopped her here, he wouldn't be bracing himself for a public reunion conducted in the small grocery store she owned and ran.

He winced at the thought. Though he'd die before he admitted it, the big, confident, supremely in command Cabe McClain had a shy streak in him. "Please don't let that store be full of women!" he silently beseeched as he began the drive back to town.

The road he traveled followed the curving coastline. Below him, the colorful speedboat flowing across a sparkling carpet of seawater created an enticing picture. Yearning washed into his eyes and made his smile wistful. When pavement dipped to meet shore he saluted Laura with his car horn. But she didn't seem to notice.

The woman he lost sight of as the road turned inland was too absorbed in her thoughts to notice much of anything, even the gradual increase in water traffic. A sharp blast from an oncoming yacht jolted Laura Richards to alertness. Moving out of the larger boat's path, she focused her pensive gaze on the old stone beacon that marked the entrance to Fair Harbor.

Had she not been in such a rush, Laura would have enjoyed her ride. The fog and drizzle that had chilled the North Carolina coast for the past week had vanished overnight, leaving behind washed blue skies and the soft, lush warmth of spring. As it was, she was bouncing across the water at an insane speed with her mind ensnarled in a tangle of worrisome thoughts.

One was the disturbing memory of the dream she'd awakened from this morning. It was a familiar dream and not all that odd: lying drowsily awake in a tangle of silken sheets, wrapped in the sensuous warmth of a lover's arms, listening to the morning sounds of a baby. Before, however, this lover was always a faceless husband. But not this time. She'd had no trouble at all recognizing the green eyes smiling down at her through spiky dark lashes. They belonged to Cabe McClain.

"Weird," she muttered, brushing back the tendrils of hair tangled in her own dark lashes. She had never so much as given a romantic thought to Cabe. Although well liked and engagingly good natured, the gangly, raw-boned youth she remembered was not considered a heartthrob even by his feminine contemporaries. To Laura, six years his junior, he had been merely another adored male pest who hung around with her equally pesty brothers.

Her puzzled frown vanished. She had gone to bed thinking about their appointment this morning, which was probably why her sleeping mind had scrambled him into her nighttime fantasies.

She'd also spent half the night studying, with drearily predictable results. The alarm hadn't gone off and she had overslept. She hadn't mentioned a word about his return to Dolly and Pearl Stewart, the two elderly aunts she'd inherited along with her store.

They were rabid matchmakers, especially Dolly. Which is why I waited until the last minute, Laura confessed to herself. I knew she'd be on me like a chicken on a June bug!

Chuckling, Laura felt a swift lift of spirits as she approached Fair Harbor. Located near the confluence of Cape Fear and the Atlantic Ocean, the picturesque little town with its color-washed cottages spilling down green bluffs shimmered like an illusion in late-April sunlight. Memories of summer vacations spent with doting grandparents made it all very real.

She and Cabe had been raised in the gentle hills just west of Wilmington, and Fair Harbor had been their playground. Another chuckle tickled her throat as she recalled the times he had been persuaded, by coaxing, pleas, or threats of tears, to take Laura, her two younger cousins and his sister Susan, to the beach. The Four Worrywarts, he had tagged them, grumbling and growling, his emerald eyes dancing as he suffered the incredible din of giggling little girls. Oh, it would be good to see him again!

Laura slowed the boat to a sedate crawl as she neared the marina, hoping, just this once, to slip in undetected. But her sleek craft was too well known to escape notice. So, apparently, was her lovelife. The silver-haired man who caught her tie-ropes greeted her with a teasingly sly, "Heard you got a handsome young buck come all the way from Raleigh just to see you, Laura!"

"Well, where did you hear that, John Ed?" Laura stopped smoothing her wind-tossed hair to ask tartly.

"He stopped to gas up that fine foreign car he's driving and Madge recognized him. The girls at the beauty shop thought he was the best looking thing to come down the road in a month of Sundays!" Marking the sharp breath Laura expelled, he hurried on, "Also heard you've got another test this afternoon. Think you can pass it this time?"

"Certainly I can," Laura said, crossing her fingers behind her back. After changing her boat shoes, she thanked him for the tie-up and cut through the busy parking lot to Main Street. From there it was only half a block to the two-story Victorian that housed Richards' Country Store.

Her hope of arriving before Cabe was proven equally futile as she spotted the apron-clad figure scudding down the walk to meet her. Just in case she hadn't been spotted, Dolly Stewart waved vigorously.

"Cabe McClain's here, Laura! We saw you come flying in. I told him to sit down and rest himself, being injured and all and I'd hurry you along. He said you were expecting him," she added accusingly.

"Yes, I am, but Aunt Dolly—"

"Why on earth didn't you say something, then? You could have knocked me down with a feather when he come walking in the door!" Dolly patted her tidy white cap of curls, blue eyes twinkling behind thin-rimmed glasses. "Hasn't he turned out fine. So tall and handsome! And polite—I don't believe I've ever met a man with nicer manners," she declared. "And obviously doing fine for himself, too. You know what he's wearing on his wrist, Laura?"

"A watch?"

"Well, yes, but not just *any* watch—and don't get sassy, Mary Laura Richards," Dolly said. "It's just as easy to love a rich man as a poor man, leastways that's what I'm told. And did you or did you not say just the other day that you wanted a family and with your botanical clock ticking away like it is—"

"That's biological clock and it's not ticking all that fast," Laura retorted, vexed at having her thoughtless words repeated for public consumption. They were passing a sidewalk café and Dolly's voice carried even when she wasn't indignant.

Crossing the lawn, Laura spoke quickly. "Now Aunt Dolly, you stop this. Cabe's a friend. His sister Susan is a friend. When she asked me to help find a rent-house for him and his little girl for the summer, naturally I said yes." She snatched a breath. "I haven't mentioned it before because I've a gorgeous house lined up for him and I couldn't chance someone else snapping it up before he got here. That's why Cabe's looking for me and that's all there is to it."

"That's all, huh?" Stopping, Dolly folded her arms across her ample bosom and made a studied appraisal of Laura's fetching appearance.

"Yes, that's all," Laura mimicked, wondering why she felt so defensive. There was a perfectly good reason for upgrading her usual workday attire of khaki culottes, plaid cotton shirt and sneakers to dark blue designer jeans iced with crisp white stitching, a sleeveless silk blouse, and high-heeled pumps.

Exasperated, she heaved a sigh as the older woman tilted her head and waited. Dolly was soft and pretty and round as a gooseberry, much like the adored grandmother Laura had lost last year.

She flung her hands up. "Oh all right, that's not all. The owners of the house are offering a lease-buy option and I've decided to try my hand at *selling* it to Cabe rather than leasing. Not only will it be good practice, but it could mean a nice bit of extra cash for us.''

Dolly's eyes rounded. "You're fixing to sell him a house? My goodness, Laura, can you do that? Well, a'course you can,'' she answered herself.

"Of course I can," Laura echoed, her doubts momentarily vanquished by Dolly's stout assurance. "And when I start my sales pitch, I don't want him seeing me as that cute little kid he used to know. I want him seeing a mature, intelligent, attractive woman. Which is why,'' she whispered as they crossed the store's front porch and stepped over Dolly's blue-eyed ginger cat, "I've taken a little extra time with my appearance!''

"Worth every minute,'' Dolly agreed. She opened the screen door. "You go on in, honey, I've got to run next door for a second.''

"All right,'' Laura said, flustered at the prospect of actually meeting Cabe again. What would he think of her? More importantly, what would she think of him? What if she didn't like him? The house she intended selling him was right next door to her apartment, which would make him her neighbor. Feeling flushed and damp and absurdly nervous, she straightened her shoulders and stepped through the doorway.

She paused just inside to adjust to the dimmer light as well as to the man who eased himself from the depths of a worn wicker rocker. Her every sense was alert and tingling as she watched his reaction to a grown-up Laura. It wasn't much. His eyes widened slightly, his mouth twitched. Piqued, she tossed him an apologetic smile that said plain as words, "Business before pleasure," and glided behind the counter to attend a waiting customer.

Cabe stood by quietly, his expression unreadable, one hand braced lightly on a shelf. Laura wanted keenly to study his face, each strong-boned contour, each shadowed hollow. She had to settle for polite glances. He was taller than

she remembered, his features more sharply defined. Those
distinctive eyes were the same, however, and the thick, wavy
cap of dark hair sweeping back from his high brow still
gleamed with auburn highlights.

The transaction completed, Laura shifted stance to permit her customer, a stoop-shouldered man with work-
scarred hands, to sign his account. He shuffled out the door
with supper in his arms; she slipped the ledger under the
counter and turned back to Cabe.

It was her first good look at him and what she saw short-
ened her breath. The lanky, graceless Cabe of her childhood no longer existed. In his place stood a man whose
powerful physique and rugged features combined to create
a dynamically attractive male.

Captivated, Laura clasped her hands behind her back and
studied him with the artlessness of a child. He had a very
masculine nose, and his dark eyebrows were perfectly
straight, except at the ends where they winged out to give
him a slightly rakish appearance. A woman's awareness
quickened her pulse as her gaze was drawn irresistibly
downward, past the enticements of wide shoulders and a
trim waist to the long, clean lines of his lower torso. He wore
his chocolate-brown slacks and cream-colored, raw silk
blazer with an air of absolute authority. The kind that took
executive power and expensive Swiss watches for granted,
she thought, noting the glint of gold encircling his wrist. The
kind, she conceded dryly, acknowledging the excitement
pulsing at her throat, that drew women like catnip draws
cats.

"Do I pass muster?" he asked, looking amused at her
lengthy scrutiny.

A mist of color tinted her sunkissed skin. She ducked her
head, then tipped it back with a throaty chuckle. "Ah yeah,
you do. More so than I expected, in fact."

He smiled and Laura wanted to fling her arms around him
much like she would greet any other old friend after a long
absence. But the awkward restraint that gripped her inhib-

ited spontaneity. Compromising, she held out a slim, unsteady hand. "Hi, Cabe. Welcome home."

Listening to the naturally husky, almost gravely voice that used to tickle him so, coming as it did from that little bit of a thing, Cabe grinned.

"Hello, Sunshine," he said.

The startled laugh Laura gave was not due entirely to the teasing use of an old nickname. Their brief clasp of fingers had ignited a tiny shower of sparks, a sensation so real that she was surprised it wasn't visible. She didn't reply for she couldn't think of anything to say. Her mind was entirely taken up with the disconcerting impact he was having on her senses.

Luckily Dolly came in scolding herself and apologizing to Cabe for not knowing that a customer had intruded upon their reunion. Her beaming smile showered over the two young people. "Well, did you two get reacquainted? Laura says you've been friends for a long time."

"A long time." A twinkle lit his eyes. "In fact, I remember her when she—"

"Ca–abe," Laura groaned. "Please don't embarrass me with that old line about remembering when I was knee high to a grasshopper."

"I wouldn't think of it," Cabe assured her. "Even though in her case it *was* an apt description," he told Dolly.

Their laughter mingled. When the door's tinkling bell shattered the moment, Laura felt a fierce pang of resentment. Two blue-haired matrons came in, trailed by a barefoot stranger. The diaper-clad baby she held clamped against one hip promptly held out its arms.

Grateful for the chance to firm up her composure, Laura took the child. "This is Sam," she said to Cabe, smiling as tiny fingers curled around her thumb.

"Hello, Sam," he said, his voice oddly husky.

Laura didn't notice. When she touched her lips to the tender spot where golden tendrils misted Sam's tender nape, longing seized her.

She wanted a baby, with an intensity that at times bordered on physical pain. She soothed her deep inner ache with the child's sweet-smelling warmth while his baby-sitter dug through cartons of used books and darted curious glances at Cabe.

When Laura also glanced his way, bewilderment knit her brow. Cabe still stood by the rocker, his gaze fastened on the baby she cuddled to her breast. The green eyes were hard, streaked with something that might have been anger or might have been pain. But when they met her questioning gaze, she saw nothing more puzzling than a glint of masculine annoyance directed at chattering females who were wasting the time of a busy man.

Imagination, she decided. She returned the child to the teenager and rolled her eyes at Dolly.

Catching the impertinent gesture, Cabe shot a pointed look at his watch to back up his small deception. He hadn't meant to show his feelings like that. The gust of bitterness had taken him completely by surprise.

So had his first close look at Laura, he admitted. When she had walked through the door he had felt absurdly stunned for the second time this morning.

Even now his normally disciplined mind kept flying on unsettling tangents. Something innocently warm and delightful tugged at his heart as he watched her. Contrarily, various unruly parts of him were embroiled in decidedly less noble feelings. That rosy mouth would be sweet to the taste, those slim, satiny fingers and the silken spill of hair cool and soft on a man's burning skin... Cabe tensed. What was he thinking—this was Laura!

"Okay, okay," she was saying and he felt another stitch in his chest as he met her dancing, sparkling dark eyes. We'll have to take your car, though. Pearl needed ours for a dental appointment this morning. Unless you'd enjoy a boat ride?"

"I think I'll pass," he returned lightly, and picked up the cane beside his chair. "Might be a little difficult getting in and out of a boat with this."

Even though his smile was hedged with prickly male pride, Dolly's good heart got the better of her. "Oh here, let me help you!"

"No," he said tersely, stopping her rush around the counter. "Thank you, I can manage."

Laura's eyes narrowed. She squeezed the older woman's shoulder and walked out the door, leaving Cabe to make it through on his own.

They were almost to the parking lot when he remarked, "I suppose Susan told you about my accident?"

"Only that you'd had one." Laura indicated the cane. "Is that going to be permanent?"

"Not the cane. Maybe a slight limp."

"A slight limp's not so bad."

"How about three inches of steel plate screwed into the bone?"

Her nose wrinkled. "In that case, I'd advise you to stay away from large magnets."

He chuckled wryly. "I'll try to keep that in mind. That's my car there, beside the travel van."

"Uh-huh, I figured it was." Flashing him a droll look, she walked around the hood of an oyster-gray Mercedes. She moved with that swingy gait so natural to sexy, narrow-legged jeans and punctuating pumps, and Cabe had to stop what he was doing to watch.

An expressive lift of her delicately curved eyebrows applauded his feat of unlocking all the doors with one twist of the key. Sliding into a luxury of smooth leather and plush carpet, Laura said cheekily, "This is going to take some getting used to, Cabe. You and that battered old pickup you used to drive seem much better suited."

His deep laugh stirred up butterflies in her midsection. He shed his blazer and got in carefully. Laura ached to help him. Instead she sat back and clasped her fingers in her lap. "Susan said you're taking the whole summer off."

"Yes. Doctor's orders; rest and heal."

"From what? Your leg injuries?"

"That, and something called burnout. I was working eighteen hours a day, seven days a week there at the end."

"Why such an obsessive schedule?"

"Because I wanted to get through with the job."

"So you burned yourself out."

"That's the prevailing theory," he said edgily.

Laura decided she wasn't up to pursuing a subject he obviously found disagreeable. Though outwardly composed, inside she twitched with nerves. Watching him stretch around to place his jacket on the back seat sent a fluid shiver down her spine. Muscles rippled and flexed beneath his thin shirt. The same coppery dark hair that dusted his arms glistened damply at the base of his throat.

Remembering, belatedly, that he did not know their destination, she managed to tell him to turn left before her attention was distracted again. His strongly carved profile fascinated her, as did his full mouth. He's a fascinating man, Laura thought, defending her acute interest in his every move. And just a little intimidating, she added in wry concession. Although the raw male power radiated by his big frame was potent enough to swamp any woman's senses, what caused her to shiver again was the air of aloof, controlled detachment stamping his features.

Settle down, Laura, she admonished herself. He's a friend, not a potential lover. But her mind was already seeking pieces to the puzzle that was Cabe McClain. She knew that he was both professionally and financially successful, that he had married and subsequently divorced the beautiful blond photojournalist he'd met in New York, that she had borne him twins and that he'd retained full custody of the surviving child, his four-year-old daughter, Heather.

But she didn't know the reasons for his divorce. Startled at the sharpness of her desire to learn them, Laura said brightly, "My goodness, how long has it been now, Cabe, twelve, thirteen years? We've got a lot of catching up to do!"

"Not really." Cabe stabbed at a button and the sunroof slid back. "I think Susan's done a pretty good job of keeping both of us up to date."

His dismissive tone stung Laura into quick agreement. After instructing him to turn left at the light, she fell silent, thinking that she would like to use the rest of the drive to sort through the thoughts crowding her mind. The blithe confidence she had displayed to Dolly was fast eroding. There was a daunting hardness about Cabe, a gloss of sophisticated cynicism, and as yet she was unable to discern how deep it went.

She cleared her throat. "Take a right here. We're going to Tulioria Manor," she said, rolling the mellifluous syllables on her tongue. "Do you remember it, that lovely old place on River Street?"

"Only vaguely. We farm boys didn't get invited all that often to places with names like Tulioria Manor," he reminded teasingly.

"Neither did a gardener's daughter—but look as us now," she said as they entered the quiet, tree-shaded street that wound between cloistered estates.

Her gleeful comment drew a chuckle from him. "I saw your place this morning. I came out early, hoping to meet you there rather than at the store."

"Oh, that's not my place, I just live on it, sort of a caretaker while the owners are in France. I'm sorry I wasn't there." Laura touched his arm, a fleeting contact that nonetheless made her acutely conscious of the warm, muscular flesh beneath her fingertips. Her voice was huskier than usual. "Sorry you had to wait for me at the store. But the manor's been closed up awhile and I wanted to open windows and air it out before you looked at it."

"Tulioria. That's an odd name," he mused. "Do you know what it means?"

"According to Mrs. Vanderhilden, it's from an ancient European dialect that roughly translates to 'a quiet place beside the river.' Personally I think she made it up, but it's lovely nevertheless. Turn here," Laura said, her smile unconsciously possessive as he drove through the brick-pillared entrance.

A wrought-iron fence ran along the street side of the parklike grounds and connected with another set of pillars that marked the exit. The lane curved behind the grove of tall pines and moss-festooned oaks that provided privacy for the double-winged, two-story house. Cabe stopped the car and sat looking around for a satisfying moment.

The trees were lush with new leaves. The air beneath the fresh green canopy was at once sultry and clean smelling, devoid of artifice, yet eminently capable of firing a man's imagination. *Like Laura,* he thought. Quickly dousing the little flame of an idea, he let his gaze wander across the wide expanse of lawn.

Pine needles covered it. Here and there enormous camellia shrubs stood as tall as saplings, their dark green shapes starred with luminous pink and white blossoms. The whole yard was alive with songbirds. As he took it all in, he felt a curiously sweet tension invading his muscles, something quite apart from, and yet very similar to, the warmth caused by Laura's brief touch.

"What do you think of it?" she asked.

"Worth a look," he said. "Those double doors are gorgeous."

Her hopes rose immediately. "That iris-patterned stained glass is an original design. Wait here a minute and I'll unlock them and then give you a hand. I should have swept this walk," she fretted, "those pine needles are going to be slippery."

Cabe didn't have time to reply; she was out of the car and up the wide steps in a flash. After unlocking the heavy doors, she hurried back to his side.

He had already set his feet to the wide rose-bricked walk. Grasping his cane, he stood up. He frowned as she caught his arm.

"Careful, Cabe, that metal tip is going to slide all over the place. You were supposed to wait until I came to help you."

"And *I* thought I'd made it plain that I don't need any help," he shot back, then mentally kicked himself as she jerked her hands from him.

"I guess you did make that plain." Her clear gaze leveled on his face. "To Aunt Dolly as well as me."

The accusation implicit in her reply stung him. "I'm sorry, Laura, I didn't mean to snap at you or Mrs. Stewart," he said quietly. But his apology wasn't enough and those dark eyes let him know it. She stared at him steadily, her back straight, her mouth set. A soft breeze had sprung up to flirt with her hair, lacing it across her nose and along the rounded flare of cheekbones.

Such an elegant face, he thought. He lifted a hand, palm up, in a gesture of helpless male contrition. It was tinged with the irritation of a man compelled to explain himself.

"It's just that after the divorce, going it alone got to be a natural state of existence with me, one I discovered I liked. And still do, I might add. Then I had an accident and found myself forced to rely upon others for every damn thing but breathing," he said roughly. "I've had six miserable months of dependency, which is why I tend to get a little testy about accepting help I don't want and don't need."

Stepping back to allow him room to maneuver, Laura kept her hands firmly in place. His outthrust chin was a touching contrast to the vulnerable set of his mouth. "You must be a strong man not to need anyone," she said, inwardly sighing as his eyes shuttered. "I wouldn't last a week without the support system Dolly, Pearl and I enjoy. All for one and one for all, that sort of thing." She shrugged, discarding the subject. "Shall we take a look inside?"

But the subject was far from discarded. So he's become a loner. Well, that won't last long, I'll see to that, she decided to herself. Backing up her thought with a decisive nod, she preceded him up the walk.

"You'll love the house, I think. I know I do..." Laura's voice faltered as she flung open the doors. Biting her lip, she gazed up the sweeping flight of stairs. This multilevel house would never do. Why hadn't she realized that the instant she saw his cane? Because you were too busy noticing the man, that's why! her conscience replied.

"Something wrong, Laura?"

"Yes, something's wrong." She sighed. Cabe had moved up behind her, so close she could smell his spicy after-shave. When he spoke, his voice vibrated throughout her entire being. Never had she been so aware of a man! Feeling hot and confused, she drew a steadying breath and turned to face him.

"I'm sorry, Cabe, I didn't even think about how you were going to get around in this house. The main living space is upstairs, and even there, the dining room, kitchen and bedrooms are two steps up from the den. It's a lovely arrangement, but not too practical for you. It wasn't that I forgot about your injury, I just didn't realize how bad it was. I apologize for wasting your time, I know you're a busy man—"

"You haven't wasted my time—and I'm not a busy man," he added with a cryptic smile. "Part of my on-going therapy is walking on different levels, good flexibility exercise for a banged-up leg. I just have to take it slow, that's all."

"But even getting around to the back of the house re-quires some climbing," she said, doggedly earnest.

A careless shrug answered her. Laura breathed easier. "Well, okay, we'll start down here. Besides the staircase in question, this floor contains a complete guest suite with a private side entrance as well as two smaller bedrooms and an oak-paneled study."

She pirouetted, her wave of hand enhancing the graceful movement. "Isn't this a lovely foyer? Parquet floors—a bit scruffy, but they'll clean up beautifully—and these handsome old ceiling fans are in every bedroom plus the den. You'd be surprised at how that cuts down on air-conditioning bills."

"I'm astonished."

"That it cuts down on air-conditioning bills?"

"No, that you said all that in one breath."

"Well. It's a gift," she said.

Amusement lightened his eyes. Laura felt her heart skip a beat. Acting on instinct, she tilted her face to his coquettishly.

With a teasing tug on her hair, he stepped around her and walked into the guest suite. Laura elected not to follow. She leaned against the smooth white banister weighing his brotherly gesture against her unsisterly urge to flirt. No more of that, Laura, you're interested in his checkbook, not his bed, she reminded herself.

But such cynicism never remained with her for long. Selling him the house was still top priority. Lord knew she needed every cent she could get her hands on and the commission the owners had offered her was sizeable. Her motivation, however, had shifted focus. She wanted to know better this tall, quiet man who was not quite friend and not quite stranger. And that task would be easy if he lived next door.

Two

After Cabe had checked the downstairs without any particular overt reaction, Laura led him upstairs to a huge den that sat like the squared bottom of a basket bordered on three sides by wide, two-tiered steps.

"Like all the rooms in this house, this one is over sized—" she gestured to the expanse of windows centered by the fireplace and flanked by French doors "—and wonderfully fresh and cool when opened to the sea breeze."

Anxiously she assessed his reaction, which was a bemused shake of head. Striving for lightness, she went on, "Those are solid oak beams, and that fireplace is native stone quarried from the Blue Ridge Mountains. The master bedroom and study are to the left, the dining room-kitchen area to the right. All overlook the river—definitely a plus point there!"

He nodded.

Feeling awkward again and not in the least sure of herself, Laura continued. "There are two more bedrooms at the far end of the right wing, making a total of six bedrooms and six and a half baths. That's not counting the servants' quarters over the garage. Behind us is an elegant formal living room. It's so light and airy—well, just see for yourself!''

Laura hurried ahead to open the white louvered doors. She waited there while Cabe reached her side, then ushered him into a delightful room with floor-to-ceiling windows, pale woods and ivory walls. His face remained impassive. Lowering her eyes lest she betray her growing frustration, she brought him to the large, sunny kitchen which, to her surprise, intrigued him. Grateful for any sign of interest, she ticked off, "Built-in double ovens, double ranges, beverage refrigerator with ice-maker, an extra large pantry."

"Nice," he murmured.

The lukewarm comment strained Laura's patience severely. He hadn't said more than two words since she'd begun showing him the house! "Very nice, I'd say. They don't build kitchens like this anymore." Having delivered her rebuke, she wheeled smartly around, and nearly bumped into the sinewy arm he had stretched across the doorframe.

Giving no sign that he'd noticed the soft press of her breasts against his arm, Cabe stepped away. "A very nice kitchen, Ms. Richards. What's next? And whatever it is, could we hurry it up a bit?"

Deriding her uneven breathing, Laura gave a clipped nod. "The master bedroom's next, then we'll go outside," she said, and walked from the kitchen, her swaying hips sensual testimony to her heightened emotions. Behind her, she heard his long exhalation, much like a suppressed groan. Concern slowed her steps. Had he overestimated himself, were all these up-and-down surfaces beginning to get to him?

"You okay?" she asked, glancing worriedly over her shoulder.

"Oh, I'm just fine, given my present state of mind," Cabe said a bit ruefully.

Now what did that mean? Laura wondered. And why did it seem such an intimacy showing him the master bedroom? Certainly his relaxed manner displayed none of the hot stiffness that kept afflicting her lissome form.

"What do you think so far?" she asked as they returned to the den.

"It has potential." His gaze flickered over her rounded hips. "Are we through with the tour?"

"No, not yet," she said edgily. Why was he in such a hurry? "What furniture's left in the house is included in the sale—"

"Whoa! Back up there—what sale?" Cabe cocked his head. "I thought we were talking lease."

"Well, yes, we were—are," she stammered. "But there's an option-to-buy included with the lease and I think you'd be a fool not to snap it up."

"You do, hmm?" he drawled. She nodded vigorously. Her color was high, her chin raised defiantly. The sudden wild rush of tenderness Cabe felt startled him. Reacting to its disquieting intensity, he shifted his weight to his good leg and clamped a hand on the arrogant jut of his hip. "What makes you think I'd want to buy a house? And here, of all places?"

"Why, because Fair Harbor's a good place to live," Laura replied, disconcerted. "And this place is a good investment, there's no doubt of that. Besides, houses like this aren't all that plentiful, which increases its value right there. Since you're considering establishing a branch office of your firm in Raleigh...well, Susan said you were," she protested the darting tilt of one dark eyebrow.

"At this point that's more Susan's wishful thinking than fact," he said dryly.

"You ought to consider it seriously then. I think it's a good idea. Anyway, this would make a perfect weekend and summer retreat. I know the house needs some minor renovating, but you have the means to do that. And it is a very smart investment, taxwise and otherwise."

Cabe smiled indulgently. "Oh? Why is that?" he murmured, feeling angry with himself because she looked so proud and vulnerable and he did want to indulge her. Which is not the act of a level-headed businessman, he mocked his overly generous urges.

Laura rummaged through her handbag and passed him a small notepad. "Because you'd be getting a bargain at twice this price," she said crisply.

After waiting a few seconds to give him time to absorb the neatly printed figures, Laura continued listing monetary facts in a competent, impersonal manner that she hoped fervently to maintain even if this was her Cabe. *My Cabe.* She could remember calling him that as a little girl, demanding to know where he was, as if he was hers to command....

Shaking off nostalgia's sweet allure, she intoned, "This is a five acre estate, with two of those acres still in their original wild state and the other two waterfront properties and thus eminently salable—"

"Laura—"

"Eminently salable because Fair Harbor's no longer a little backwater village, not with all the development around town and on the islands. Another reason for the discerning buyer's interest is that this is the only one of the few remaining landed estates being offered, either now, or in the foreseeable future—"

"Laura."

"Darn it, Cabe, will you just hush up and *listen*!" Laura exploded. "At least give me half a chance. If I didn't believe in what I'm doing, I wouldn't spend so much time and effort doing it."

"Why *are* you doing it?" Cabe asked curiously.

Laura overruled sentiment in favor of intellect. "For several reasons. One's financial. This is a favor to the owners, but there's also a bit of cash in it for me. Another is that I'm studying to be a realtor, and gaining some first-hand exposure can't hurt."

Cabe's eyebrows shot up. "You, a realtor?"

His skepticism didn't affront her; Laura figured he had good reason. He had been one of her math tutors in high school. "I know. I'm not exactly crazy about the idea, but it seems practical since it's something I can work in with managing the store."

She tore off the fact sheet and gave it to him. "The other reason is you, Cabe. You and this house have very similar needs, I think. It's a happy house, you can feel that as soon as you walk in. But it needs a family," she said, her eyes as soft as her voice. "It needs a husband and wife loving each other, kids and puppies and kittens underfoot."

Cabe's studied amusement masked the bitter hurt that winced through him. A family? He'd had that once. He refused to hope that he'd have it again. Hope was dangerous. Hope could slice up a man like a razor.

"I hardly think one man and a little girl make a family," he rebutted mildly. "Not the kind you're talking about, at any rate."

"It won't always be just one man and a little girl."

"Now how would you know a thing like that?"

She tossed her head. "Sometimes you just know these things."

Despite her lighthearted tone, Laura felt an echo of the same wistfulness that had shadowed Cabe's eyes creep into hers. What she had prescribed for the house was exactly what she wanted for herself.

When he spoke again, his voice was neutral. "I doubt you have any idea what I need, but all right, Laura, I'm listening."

Laura stiffened. "Sorry, I didn't mean to presume." Opening the nearest set of French doors, she suggested, "Shall we take a look out back? This flagstone terrace runs the full length of the house and surrounds the pool."

Sensing rather than seeing that Cabe had stepped outside with her, she tensed up again. "There are several outbuildings down that slope . . . if you'd like to see them?"

"In a minute. First I'd like to find out if I'm just imagining things or if you feel awkward with me. Personally, I mean, not with this house business. Do you?" he prodded as she plucked a sprig of yellow jasmine and inhaled its fragrance.

"There's some strain," Laura admitted. "There shouldn't be, but there is. Maybe because I keep realizing we're no longer kids." Her lips quirked awry. "Also maybe because you've grown into one of the most attractive men I've ever met and I'm having a little trouble adjusting to that."

To her delight, Cabe reddened. "You've grown up nicely yourself." Studying her flushed face, he set down his cane, his smile tender. "Neither of us are kids anymore, but we're still Laura and Cabe. And you're still my Sunshine. Come here," he ordered huskily, holding out his arms.

His hug was accepted without hesitation; Laura was dying to know the feel of his arms around her. As they enfolded her, she had to close her eyes to cope with the deluge of wildly conflicting sensations.

Standing in the loose circle of his embrace made her feel indescribably secure and protected. What his nearness was doing to her nervous system was something altogether different. Instinctual caution urged her to stay within the safe boundaries of their former relationship, at least until she had learned what kind of man he'd become. But it was difficult to ignore the fact that she was being held by a handsome, virile male and not some adolescent memory. His strong arms made a delicious nest for her body. There was an exciting tenderness in the big hands spreading slowly across her back. One moved upward and molded the shape of her head, pressing her face into the dusky vee of his open collar.

The low, strained laugh he uttered vibrated against the puckered tips of her breasts. Marveling that so much feeling could come from a casual hug, she looked up at him, her eyes wide and lips softly parted.

Cabe's fingers loosened on her head and slid into the mane of golden brown hair. A gasp escaped her lips as he slowly leaned down to her. Hot bursts of sensation weakened her knees alarmingly as she waited, quivering, for the kiss they both had to have. His warm breath bathed her face. His mouth touched hers with the delicacy of a butterfly lighting on a blossom. Then he released her.

They were standing beside a low brick retaining wall. Not yet trusting her legs, Laura was thankful for the solid surface beneath her outspread hand. She felt gloriously chagrined. Cabe's hug and kiss were exactly what he meant them to be, gentle, brotherly gestures. Yet those shooting-star sensations still sizzled through her body.

Her other hand, she discovered, was stroking his taut-muscled arm. When he glanced downward, she pulled back her errant fingers and stared at them as if mystified by their action. More self-conscious than ever, she said on a nervous laugh, "Well, that was nice!"

"Yes," he said simply. With indolent ease he propped a booted foot on the low stone wall. "I'm going out to Thackary Island for a while this afternoon. Want to come along?"

Wickedly tempted, Laura bit her lip. "I can't, Cabe. Along with that realty seminar, I'm taking courses at the junior college and my whole afternoon's filled with classes." She brightened. "But we could have lunch. I might even be able to wangle us two of the scrumptious sandwiches Aunt Dolly makes up each day for a few lucky regulars. You hungry?"

"I'm hungry. And willing, except..." Cabe tilted his head, mock-wary. "This isn't going to be one of your dreaded tea parties, is it?"

Laura knew immediately what he meant. Laughter tickled her throat as an incongruous image popped to mind, a long-legged Cabe and her two husky brothers scrunched up around a tree-stump table holding the tiny handles of miniature teacups, pinkies properly extended as instructed by their bossy little hostess.

As green eyes and dark shared the memory, an old, steadfast affection gushed up through the murky confusion. This time Laura didn't have to wonder if he felt what she did. With a grin that could stop a woman's heart, Cabe swept her up in an exuberant, one-armed embrace. She clung to his broad shoulder with both hands while they shared a laugh that shattered constraint and dampened their interlocked gazes.

This is the way it should be, Laura thought happily.

This is the way it will be, Cabe vowed.

He set her down with exaggerated care. Laura sorted through her healthy store of questions. Extracting one that seemed harmless enough, she asked, "You own other homes, don't you?"

"No. Well, the New York apartment, but it's being sublet right now."

"Nothing else?"

"A beach duplex on Maui, I'm nuts about beaches. A ski lodge in Austria and one in Vail—I'm also a ski freak. Or was. A corporate ranch in Wyoming—" Cabe caught himself up short, abashed to realize he was betraying his almost boyish delight in the transition from blue-collar farmstock to a man of means. "But those are just drop-in places, not homes."

Laura's ironic smile turned inward as she listened to his careless recital of the kind of life she knew nothing about. *The minute I start thinking, good old Cabe, he shows me a side of himself that knocks all my preconceptions awry.* "Mercy," she said faintly. "A ski lodge in Vail is impressive enough, but one in Austria, too?"

"Investments." Satisfied with his succinct explanation, Cabe picked up his discarded cane. "What's the perfume you're wearing?" he asked, a thoughtless question, and one he immediately regretted, especially since it turned out that she wasn't wearing perfume. But he couldn't blame himself for feeling so rattled as she moved from him.

"If you could bottle the way you smell you'd make a fortune," he remarked, collecting his cane. "What's in Dolly's scrumptious sandwiches?"

Ridiculously glad that she'd run out of perfume, Laura drew a long breath. "Today is barbecued brisket from her prize-winning recipe, served on homemade bread with slices of Beefsteak tomatoes from a friend's greenhouse."

"Lets go."

"Right now? But you haven't seen everything yet."

"My stomach says I've seen enough." He grinned. "You may take my arm if you'd like."

"Well, if you're sure I won't be insulting your macho male image..." Ignoring his scowl, she slipped a hand under his elbow and started them down the wide, stepped path. "When are you returning to Raleigh?"

"This afternoon."

"Oh." Struggling with disappointment, Laura advised herself to be sensible. A man didn't buy a house in one day's time. But he could lease it.

"Cabe, this rental offer does have a time limit."

"I'm aware of that, Laura."

Laura didn't pursue it. Though he spoke quietly the message came through loud and clear. He was not a man to be pushed. But oh, she wanted to push! "Just making sure," she replied lightly.

After she had locked up, they drove back to town at an easy pace. "I didn't know Dolly was your aunt," he said, opening up a comfortable line of conversation.

"Technically, she's not. Neither is Pearl. I just adopted them, although Dolly is distantly related to me somewhere down the line. They're sisters-in-law, both widows. Both about as sophisticated as tulips," she said with a fond chuckle.

Sensing his interest, Laura expanded her description. The two women lived above the store and helped out in it to defray expenses. In her spare time Pearl painted—charmingly primitive landscapes which, on sunny Saturdays, Laura hung outside on a fence along the town's main street, to be bought by the occasional tourist—and watched for UFOs. Dolly did needlework and watched out for Pearl.

A smile had relaxed his mouth. Laura's fingers came to rest atop the hand he kept on the gearshift. "They're lovely people. So's your daughter, Cabe," she said, pronouncing his name with an unconsciously soft, caressing note. "I guess you know she and I are acquainted?"

He shook his head, causing a lustrous dark lock to fall over his brow. Fighting an urge to brush it back in place, she continued, "I spent my last three months in Raleigh working at the nursery school she attended. With Susan and Pete on vacation I'm surprised you didn't bring her with you. Who's watching her while you're gone?"

Cabe glanced at her, his eyes hooded. His body was still reacting to the sound of his name spoken in that velvety voice.

Wrenching his mind back to her question, he said tersely, "Our mutual friends, Juliet and Cord Hunter, are staying at the house while Susan's in the Bahamas. Since this is the last leg of a three-day business trip, I thought Heather would be better off at home."

Laura swallowed the rest of her questions. When they reached the store she took him in through the back gate and settled him on the wide wisteria-hung veranda before going inside to get their food.

There were still a few of the noontime crowd standing around joshing with each other, dockhands, mostly, though a suit-clad businessman could be seen trying to balance a soft drink and a sandwich without spotting his tie. She waved at them and slid behind the glass-fronted display cooler where Dolly stood slicing the remaining brisket.

"Cabe's out on the porch, Aunt Dolly. We're having lunch there, so I'll need two sandwiches. I'll fix them my-self—"

"Oh nonsense, I'll do the fixing. No sense letting Cabe sit out there alone," Dolly stated. "Besides, Pearl just got home and she's dying to meet him."

As if by magic, the woman she spoke of materialized around the corner of the cooler to stand beside her. Laura's stern expression began to crumble as she looked from Dolly's sweet, unadorned face with its nimbus of silvery hair, to the triangular one that sported lipstick and eye shadow. Pearl didn't believe in gray hair. *Her* fluffy cap of curls was beige-blond.

Slim as a reed and given to lace-edged blouses and soft, full skirts, she was the picture of a faded Southern belle, which she had never been. Her parents were Georgia share-croppers. But Laura would have made short work of anyone who ridiculed Pearl's pretty ways and the endearingly grand airs she put on.

"Hi, honey," she greeted Laura, "My goodness, don't you look gorgeous—all lit up like a Fourth of July sparkler! But no wonder, selling your very first house—and to an old friend, too!"

"Hi yourself," Laura said, adding an extra squeeze to her reciprocal hug. "And thank you, but I'm a long way from selling my old friend anything. Aunt Dolly—"

"Pearl, lend me a hand here," Dolly said quickly. "We're fixing Cabe and Laura some lunch."

Laura gave in. "But you behave yourself, you hear? Those knowing looks you kept throwing at Cabe and me earlier weren't appreciated at all."

"Well, of course they weren't. Really, Dolly," Pearl scolded, "Laura's got more beaus now than she can shake a stick at! None of them worth the tip of her little finger, but..." Hearing Laura's long sigh, she patted the young woman's rosy cheek. "Don't worry, honey, you won't hear a peep out of her when we bring those sandwiches. What you want to drink? Beer?"

"Yes, two beers," Laura said rather despairingly.

She and Cabe were sitting in the old wooden glider, rocking and idly chatting when their food arrived. His appreciative first bite of the fragrant sandwich, followed by a swig of icy beer and a satisfied "Ahh," brought warm smiles all around.

"When were you born, Cabe?" Pearl inquired. "I need the month, date and hour."

"Pearl's an astrology buff," Laura explained. Still looking bemused, he provided the information, which Pearl accepted with a pleased nod.

When Cabe announced that he could not, in good conscience, remain seated while the ladies stood, they immediately made themselves comfortable in lawn chairs. Laura tried to forestall the inevitable reminiscing by wondering aloud who was minding the store.

"John Ed is," Dolly said. A moment later she and Pearl were regaling Cabe with humorous anecdotes concerning Laura's adolescence.

Cabe's pleasure was genuine. Anything having to do with Laura interested him. But what he was enjoying most was the chance to study her openly. How lovely she was, he marveled. When did the braces come off and the glasses vanish? When had plain brown eyes turned into captivating dark stars fringed with even darker lashes? And how did a scruffy ponytail evolve into a cloud of loose, silken curls that tumbled or bounced or swayed or swirled— that did anything but lie passively on her shoulders?

Just watching her lips close around the narrow brown neck of a beer bottle flooded him with a riotous confusion of feelings. She seemed as innocent and wholesome as a mountain apple and undoubtedly was, yet every inch of her radiated sexuality.

Smiling to absolve his blatant stare, he watched her pop a succulent red morsel of tomato into her mouth, followed by the tip of her tongue swirling over her upper lip to capture a fleck of creamy mayonnaise.

In unconscious mimicry, he licked his lips. His tongue tasted beer and not the sweetness it hungered for. He polished off the rest of his sandwich, then glanced pointedly at his watch.

Taking the hint, the two older women remembered they had a store to run. Musingly Cabe said to Laura, "I'll have an hour or two to spare before I head back to Raleigh. If you don't mind giving me the house key, I'd like to take a private look at the place."

"Of course I don't mind. And if I'm not home when you finish, just leave the key under the Welcome mat."

Standing, Laura went through her pockets until she found the key.

Cabe took it, then flexed his long legs and stood up. "Listen, you said you needed money—"

"I said no such thing!"

"Let me reword that," he proposed, discovering himself impaled upon her indignant dark gaze. "If you should, by any chance, find yourself in need of a loan . . ."

"Thank you, but I won't." Laura hadn't meant to speak so curtly. "True, we're broke," she confided puckishly, "but around here being broke is an honorable estate. We're doing fine, Cabe. But thanks, anyway."

Cabe countered by thanking her for a very satisfying lunch and for the trouble she had gone to on his behalf. She walked him to the gate, slowly, accommodating his uneven gate. A muscle in his jaw ticked—how he'd like to stride along beside her with his old, arrogant grace!

Softly, she asked, "Cabe? How did your accident happen?"

"It involved a crumbling cliff and the piece of heavy machinery I was driving across it at the time." They had reached the gate. He paused. "Sure you can't play hooky this afternoon?"

Laura laughed and waved him down the walk. It was unsettling how much she had wanted to say yes—to anything he asked.

Three

___

Evening sunlight was burnishing the river by the time Cabe returned the house key to Laura. He stayed but a moment, and spent that on the porch. She was barefoot, dressed in a simple white cotton frock, her hair piled atop her head in charming disarray. The ache of desire he had felt this morning suddenly sharpened. She looked as fragile as lace and as much as it irked him to admit it, he didn't trust this tired, needful self he had brought back to her doorstep. So he stayed on the porch.

She raised both arms to tuck in a loosened curl, her pose unconsciously seductive as she asked, "It's still early yet, Cabe. You sure you don't have time for a drink?"

"No," Cabe said, forcing the word out. He couldn't remember the last time he'd wanted a woman this badly! "I'm beat, it's a long drive home and I just want to get it over with. But thank you, Laura. For everything."

Murmuring a shy "You're welcome," she stretched up on tiptoes to bestow a goodbye kiss on his cheek. Whether by accident or design Cabe couldn't say, but he turned his head just then and her soft mouth met his with enchanting perfection.

The contact, though brief, had an astonishing effect on his senses. Cabe felt his knees weaken and his head take a dizzying spin at the wild clash of desires. The temptation to abandon restraint was unbelievably strong. So was his aversion to violating an innocent goodbye kiss. His lips remained closed despite his urge to plunge into the sweetness of her mouth.

She drew back and looked up at him, her eyes at once sultry and vulnerable. Cabe was immediately assailed by two deep, primal urges. He wanted to make love to her with hot-blooded disregard for the consequences. Contrarily, his hands balled into fists as he considered the pleasure of dealing with anyone who brought pain to those beautiful eyes. That includes you, McClain, he admonished himself. You're not messing up her life.

With a quick laugh she smoothed her dress, which didn't need smoothing. Cabe felt another urge to do something intensely physical. Like rush out and slay a dragon, he thought, wry-lipped.

"Cabe, it was so good seeing you again," she said very softly. "Whatever you decide about the house, don't be a stranger, you're more than welcome around here. Tell Heather hello for me?"

"Yes, I will. Good night, Mary Laura," Cabe replied, and left before he did something foolish.

Once he reached the highway, Cabe set his mind on the woman he had left so reluctantly. He was relieved Laura had not pressed him for a decision on the house, for he had made none. It was impossible to decide anything until he had regained a measure of objectivity. A thrill twisted through his nerves each time he recalled the electrifying taste of her soft mouth, the feel of her supple body as he'd held her. How sweet she was, this woman who had come to him from the girl of yesterday....

Abashed to realize he had nearly run a red light, Cabe shook off his erotic bemusement. "Regaining a measure of self-discipline might not be a bad thing either," he chastised himself dryly.

Cabe's pride in the uncompromising will that had served him so well in the past proved justified. By the time he arrived at his sister's home, he had managed to put his reaction to Laura into comfortable perspective.

Nothing odd about it, he summed up. Just natural affection mixed with automatic male response to an appealing woman—and to the status he'd given her, he added. Would she have been nearly so alluring had not his personal code of conduct labeled her off limits? He doubted it. There was nothing as irresistible as forbidden fruit, he thought cynically.

A few minutes later he sat in the serenity of a cherry-wood-paneled den enjoying a much needed drink with his dear friends, Juliet and Cord Hunter. Between sips of very good brandy, Cabe answered questions about his trip, the house, Laura, and Fair Harbor's investment potential with undeviating matter-of-factness.

Growing impatient with the prolonged business discussion, Juliet summarily changed subjects. Cabe eyed her with fond exasperation as he admitted that Laura had grown into a beauty, that he didn't know what he was going to do about the house and that, yes, he was hungry.

Satisfied, Juliet ordered a tray for him, then excused herself to attend her infant son's ten o'clock feeding.

Cord decided he'd go with her. "There's only our nursemaid and Susan's nanny to help handle such a tremendous task," he explained solemnly.

As he spoke, he slid a caressing hand up her arm. After two years of marriage his love and desire for his wife was still shamelessly obvious. As for Juliet, the aura of being well-loved that cloaked her slender form was as tangible as the happiness glowing in her sapphire eyes.

"You're only playing it cool because Cabe's here," she sniffed. "Otherwise it would be a race to see who gets to the baby first."

Cabe frowned. "Woman, you're forgetting your place again," he warned, his voice breaking with laughter as she gave him a haughty look that would have chopped down a lesser man.

Watching them together made Cabe's heart hurt. To have a woman look at him that way! he thought with raw envy. Or more to the point, to be the kind of man who could afford it, he amended. But you can't, he reminded himself flatly. Not with this messed-up head you can't.

Sighing, he ran his fingers through his hair. He wished he was the sort of man who took what he wanted without a thought for the woman involved.

But he was essentially an old-fashioned man with an outmoded code of honor. Although it had been over two years since he and Michele had ended their marriage, thoughts of their shattered union yet evoked a confusing swirl of emotions. Anger, bitterness, hurt, the amorphous sense of betrayal; these unreasoning ghosts from the past were still strong, still capable of tainting his relationship with other women.

Consequently he avoided anything but the most shallow involvement. Dumping his mixed-up emotions on an unsuspecting woman was hardly the act of a gentleman.

Cabe was anything but gentle on himself. It embarrassed him that he could not shrug off a failed marriage with the fashionable ease displayed by other men. But he had loved his bright, intense, idealistic wife too much to rush into a divorce. He'd waited and hoped she'd reshuffle her priorities. It had taken him six months just to file the papers.

Did other men take divorce as badly as he had? Perhaps not. But his sad tale had an odd twist to it....

A sudden shiver took him. Struggling to counteract the strange, angry melancholy that swept over him, Cabe propped up his leg and concentrated on the bracing discomfort of a deep, rough massage until his dinner arrived. He ate hungrily, hoping the rich food would fill his inner emptiness, knowing that nothing could.

The housekeeper came for the tray and left a stack of mail. Cabe's features sharpened as he picked up a beige and blue-bordered envelope. Michele's stationery. Opening it, he read the message with utter lack of expression. She wanted to take Heather for two weeks in July. He tossed the letter back on the mail tray. As far as he was concerned it didn't even rate a reply, but for Heather's sake, civility was called for.

The letter deepened his disturbing mood. It had been a long time since he'd reflected upon his life with Michele and he really didn't care to do so now. But there seemed no way to stop it. Resignedly he closed his eyes and continued his somber flow of thought.

He had never felt totally secure with Michele's restless, quicksilver nature. With an innocence that later made him flinch, he had thought children would stabilize their union and was delighted at the prospect of becoming a father, and very nearly euphoric when they were told to expect twins. It was, however, a wretched pregnancy, and a difficult, life-threatening birth.

Although small, the twins were healthy, and Michele recovered rapidly. But they dared not risk another pregnancy.

A vasectomy seemed the simplest way to ensure that. Cabe had the usual queasy male feelings about surgical interference with this most intimate part of his body. But he had mastered his fears and made the decision freely. He had everything he wanted.

Until his tiny son became a victim to what the doctor termed "infant crib death."

Until Michele's growing discontent confirmed what she had suspected all along, that she wasn't cut out to be the wife he wanted.

She felt trapped. She wanted the freedom to travel, for however long her career demanded. And the man she wanted to travel with was the attractive, internationally known author and wildlife conservationist who had just honored her with a fulltime position on his staff.

Intellectually, Cabe knew she had not betrayed him. Michele's moral code was as strong as his. She had not been unfaithful. But he still felt betrayed.

He likewise knew that the fiery outrage that consumed him had no rational basis. But damn it, he had subjected an intimate part of his masculinity to a surgeon's knife for her. He could remind himself that it was his choice until he was blue in the face, he still felt outraged.

In the end, he had engaged a lawyer, obtained unrestricted custody of his two-year-old daughter, and installed her and his longtime housekeeper in an apartment overlooking Central Park. Five months later he was in Brazil working on a dam his firm was building.

The latter proved to be a very wise decision. Hard physical and mental labor coupled with crude living conditions stripped a man's needs to the barest essentials. For months he did little more than work, eat, and sleep, a Spartan routine that perfectly suited his savage mood.

Midway through his stay, his housekeeper's allergies forced her to retire to a son's Arizona home. Cabe had to turn his daughter over to his sister until his project was completed. But his accident had prevented him from personally seeing the product to its finish.

The sound of raised voices terminated his joyless trip into the past. Distinguishing his daughter's petulant wail, Cabe hurried upstairs.

Juliet met him in the hallway. "What's wrong?" he asked sharply.

"Nothing serious," she was quick to reassure him. "For the past two nights Heather's been stealing into your room to sleep and I just discovered her there again. When I tried to move her back to her own room we had an argument, which she won, of course.''

Letting a smile acknowledge her rueful confession, Cabe directed his uneven steps past his daughter's empty bedroom to the one he used. Heather lay propped up on his pillows, her small hands clamped on the covers drawn up to her chin.

Her mouth was a soft pout of defiance, her big green eyes fixed warily on his face. "Heather," Cabe growled, exasperated at the tenderness melting his stern frown, "what's this I hear about you giving Juliet trouble?" Leaning over, he smoothed her dandelion-silk hair. "You have a bed of your own, why are you in mine?"

"You were gone."

"True. But now I'm here. You knew that. So why wouldn't you go back to your own bed?"

"Because."

Cabe tried another frown. "Not good enough. Because why?"

"Because you might not be here when I wake up!" the little girl burst out. "You might go away again."

"Heather." He sat down on the bed. "Honey, I was only gone two nights. I wouldn't call that going away."

"But once you did go away." Tears sparkled on the lashes she lowered against her father's tightening expression. "You went away and left me for a long, long time," she said in a quavery little voice that pierced Cabe's heart like a stiletto. He'd had no idea she felt so insecure.

"Because I had to, love," he replied huskily, struggling against the confused guilt. Was he such a bad father? Where did his duty to himself begin and end—where was the dividing line between parent and man? Feeling helpless and inept, he rubbed his face and released a tired sigh.

"Oh, Daddy, I'm sorry. I didn't mean to hurt your feelings," Heather choked, peeking at him through her fingers.

"No, baby, of course you didn't." Cabe held out his arms and she lunged into them.

His gut tightened. Absently he stroked her hair. "I did leave you once, but it won't happen again. That I promise you. Maybe a business trip now and then—" his expression became thoughtful, "—or when I'm doing something that's going to be wonderful for both of us. But never longer than a week. And you'll know before I leave, the exact day I'm coming home. That's another promise. So there!"

Growling like a bear, Cabe pretended to bite her neck. She giggled. Oh God, let me do this right! he prayed silently. "Someone told me you like surprises. Is that really true?" he asked skeptically.

The head on his shoulder bobbed vigorously. "Well, okay! If you can stop all this sniffling and sit up like my big girl, I just might find one for you."

Cabe laughed as she bounced out of his arms and onto her knees, her damp face lifting indignantly. "I *am* your big girl, Daddy. You just weren't here to see me getting big is all."

"Well, there's nothing wrong with being my little girl at times, either. Here. Blow," he ordered, swaddling her snub nose in his handkerchief. Obediently she blew into it. "That's better," he approved. "Now for the surprise. Do you remember Miss Richards, Miss Laura Richards?"

"Oh, yes, Daddy, she was my favorite teacher in the whole world!" The shining green eyes he looked into dulled. "But she went away, too."

"Because she had to, honey. Sometimes people do," he reminded gently. "How would you like to see her again?"

Watching her small face light up, Cabe stilled as Laura's soft, throaty voice whispered through his head. *A quiet place beside the river.* And a woman who lingers on the mind like a beautiful melody, he added in silent warning. But he was a strong man.

He took a deep breath. "Even better than that, how would you like to spend the summer living right next door to her?"

The store smelled fragrantly of hot coffee and applecake when Laura came in early the next morning. The aunts were enjoying a leisurely breakfast that she needed no urging to join. Pearl brought up the subject of the horoscope she had cast for Cabe.

"He's a Scorpio with his moon in Cancer, which means he's the type of man who feels deeply, commits himself deeply and thus can be deeply hurt—"

"And he's loving, caring, nurturing and generous-hearted," Dolly chimed in. "A natural-born family man if ever there was one!" She pinkened at Laura's smile. "Or so Pearl says. I don't put much stock in horoscopes myself. But if there's any truth at all in that, he's a jewel of a catch. Slice me off another chunk of that cake, Pearl. Any news on the house, Laura?" she threw in casually.

"Dolly, it's way too early to know anything yet," Pearl chided. She picked up her cup and saucer, pinkie delicately arched, and sipped. "But Cabe'll be back, I'd bet on it. I saw the way he looked at you, honey," she said to Laura. "I'm an expert at things like that."

"You're an expert all right, but with you, we're talking armies, not individuals," Dolly sniffed.

Pearl jingled her bangles. "Why, Dolly Stewart! Are you saying I'm promiscuous?"

"Goodness, no," Dolly said. "Just well traveled."

Laura grinned to herself as Pearl straightened her pearls, her icy Southern accent thick enough to spread on toast. "There is nothing wrong with a little clean, honest, affectionate lust, Dolly. Having a fun-loving spirit is all part of staying young. It is also, I might point out, a part of nature. Every creature on this earth is gifted with it. Even toads—I've never seen so many little bitty toads as I have lately. You think there'd be near as many if they had the

same priggish attitude as you? But I suppose you can't help
it." With delicious magnanimity, she pat-patted Dolly's
hand. "Being stuck in the fifties' frame of mind as you are."

"And I suppose you can't help being off a half a bubble," Dolly retorted. Tossing her head, she put on her apron
and went to open the store.

"I have to admit you have an intriguing philosophy, Aunt
Pearl," Laura murmured, thinking of the excitement Cabe
had aroused with that little do-nothing kiss.

Pearl's all-over grin broke out. "And a sensible one, too.
Your Cabe proves that point. There's something warm and
sparkly between you and that good-lookin' man, Mary
Laura, something that demands respect whatever name you
give it. And him being sweet and sensitive to boot—if you
don't take what he's got to offer first chance you get, you're
no kin of mine!"

Laura had to embrace her twinkly-eyed little aunt. How
could Cabe not need this kind of loving support? she wondered fiercely. Stepping away, she put on her pink smock,
sighing. "That's what's so bad about intriguing philoso-
phies, they always belong to someone else. But I'll keep your
suggestion in mind should Cabe decide to return to our fair
town."

The next few days passed at a snail's pace. Laura heard
nothing from Cabe. "Cabe will call when he has something
to call about," she shushed her aunts, a sensible remark that
did absolutely nothing for her own inner agitation.

Friday was ordinarily her day off, but she felt too restless
to lie about. After quick-cleaning her three-rooms-and-bath
cottage, she decided to work at the store until her two
o'clock classes.

The mail had come. Laura took it to the back room that
served as an office. Most of it was bills, she noted with the
usual twinge of anxiety. Bills with a no-grace period. Richards' Country Store was not considered a good credit risk.
That was also a fair estimation of her inheritance, she

thought wryly. Her grandmother had left an appalling tangle of unpaid bills and back taxes.

Laura had used every resource she possessed to deal with her acquired debts, from seeking a second mortgage on the land and building—only to learn that one already existed—to exhausting her own savings. Her efforts fell far short of adequacy.

Richards' had been in existence for nearly a century. She didn't want to be the one to lose it! But I don't know what else to do, she fumed, writing checks and stuffing them into envelopes. We work our buns off trying to keep this place going, and for what? All we're doing is treading water, we're not getting anywhere.

"Hi, honey, what you doing?" Pearl asked, sticking her head inside the door.

"Having a pity party," Laura said.

That evening, driven by energy she had to release or explode, Laura piled her hair atop her head, changed her sweater and skirt to shorts and a big shirt, and went to work in her garden.

Through the trees she could see the manor's dark red roof, which stirred up thoughts of Cabe to add to her edginess. How did he really feel about her? Was she merely the fondly remembered sister of an old school friend? She'd much prefer a light touch of that affectionate lust Aunt Pearl spoke of.

The admission increased her agitation and she was raking leaves with abandon when a little girl burst through the hedge separating the two properties. Laura dropped the rake with a gasp of delighted surprise. With those sparkling green eyes and that Alice-in-Wonderland hairstyle, there was no mistaking Heather McClain!

"Miss Richards, guess what!" she called as she flew across the lawn.

"What?" Laura responded laughingly, her eyes searching behind the running child.

"I'm going to be your neighbor! Daddy says this is going to be our home for the whole summer and just as soon as he gets the house fixed up he'll bring me here to live with him." Heather gulped a breath as she rocketed to a stop in front of Laura. "And then we'll be good friends and neighbors, he says! Oh, Miss Richards!"

"Oh, Heather!" Laura responded. Kneeling, she draped her arms loosely around the excited child's waist. "That's wonderful news, honey. But I..." she stopped, her breath drying up as two long legs planted themselves behind Heather.

"But I wasn't told about any of this," she finished slowly, her gaze moving up Cabe's lean physique to impact with his heart-stopping grin.

Looking relaxed and handsome in a navy-blue shirt and trousers, he rocked back on his heels, bedeviling green eyes roaming over her disheveled hair and rag-tag gardening clothes.

"You're looking mighty fetching, Mary Laura," he said, veiling the truth in a teasing drawl. Those fraying denim shorts displayed a blood-stirring amount of skin. "You weren't told about it because I gave orders not to. I wanted to tell you myself. In person." His grin widened. "Surprised?"

"Well, yes I am, Cabe, but I—"

"And pleased?"

"Yes, that, too," Laura replied, astonishing herself with the just-right tone she had managed to produce from a constricted throat. "You really are taking the house?"

Cabe caught her hand and pulled her up beside him. Her tapered fingers were tipped with gently pointed nails. He didn't consciously imagine them raking down a man's back in the heat of passion. The image was just there.

His expression became impassive as he dropped her hand. "We really are. In fact, I'm having some appliances delivered tomorrow, and more furniture arriving the early part of next week."

Laura's mind spun. Everything was happening too fast! "But you can't buy a house this fast, can you?"

His teeth flashed. "You can if you pay cash."

"Oh." Mischief suddenly glinted in her eyes. "Yes, of course, I forgot. One who pays cash doesn't have to worry about such tiresome things as negotiating price and points and bank loans!"

This time Cabe's grin was a tiny bit sheepish. Laura laughed, pleased that he wasn't blasé about having money. She diverted her gaze to his daughter, who stood transfixed by the sight of a saucy squirrel. "Heather, if you'll run over and open the back door, a little dog will come rushing out and follow that squirrel right up a tree," she declared.

Heather quickly obeyed.

"I'm not real sure that's a dog, but I am sure that dogs don't climb trees," Cabe said, eyeing the tiny silver schnauzer racing at breakneck speed toward them with Heather hot on its heels.

"Of course that's a dog. KK has a pedigree a mile long," Laura replied haughtily, but she spoiled it by laughing. A little black nose and a little red tongue in a little round ball of fur—that's all there was to KK.

"Squirrel, KK," she called, pointing. Without a break in his furious yapping, the dog streaked off after the squirrel. When the smaller animal ran up a tree, KK was right behind it.

"I'll be damned," Cabe decided. "How'd he do that?"

"He and the squirrel play this game all the time and I figure he gets so caught up in it that he simply forgets he can't climb. Anyway, that tree grows *out* more than *up*, so that provides leverage." Laura chuckled again and touched his bare arm, her pulses quickening. "The only problem is that KK knows how to get up, but not down!"

After rescuing the stranded but not overly concerned animal, she placed it in Heather's care and sauntered back to the cottage where Cabe stood leaning against the railing of her minuscule porch.

"Have you and Heather had dinner?" Cabe shook his head. "Me neither. I'd offer to cook something but I don't cook. It's a family tradition," she told him. "Mom never cooked, either. But we could order pizza?"

Heather came racing back. "Please, Daddy, say yes, *please*?"

He frowned. "Heather, remember what I said about not being a bother while we're here?"

"Cabe," Laura sighed. "That's what friends *do*— bother. Around here it's practically a law. Also a pleasure. Besides, the only thing I considered doing this evening was dropping in on a beach party."

Cabe narrowed his eyes. "Laura, if you want to go," he began impatiently.

"Are you kidding? Spend the evening on some sandy beach when I can have pizza with you guys?" Laura asked incredulously. Her manner, like her voice, was too bright, but she felt fizzy-brained with happiness and excitement.

The two McClains laughed and she savored the sound. When Heather proclaimed her immense satisfaction with their dinner plans, Cabe stopped her with a stern, "That's enough, Heather. Remember what else I said?"

"Oh, yeah. Daddy wants to take you out and leave me with a baby-sitter," Heather remembered, scowling.

"With a very special baby-sitter," Cabe reminded.

Her little face cleared and she nodded vigorously. "She's your Aunt Dolly," she told Laura, "and she *really likes* little girls." She pinned her green gaze on her father. "Especially good little girls like me," she added, obviously a rebuttal to an earlier disagreement on proper behavior.

"Humph." Cabe grinned and turned to forestall Laura's question. "I stopped by on the way over here to see if Mrs. Stewart would be interested, and she and Heather got on famously. I'll pay her, of course."

"Of course."

Her suspiciously sweet tone curled his mouth again. "About that date," he said gruffly. "Since you have nothing special planned and since I dislike owing favors as well as being considered a tactless ingrate, I would like to take you to dinner. Anywhere you want to go."

"Oh, Cabe, you don't have to do that . . ." She paused, intrigued. "Anywhere?"

"Anywhere."

"Well, you do owe me a favor—but pizza here will be just fine . . . although I would love to get all dressed up and go to some romantic, candlelit restaurant—" She stopped and gave him a pained look as quiet laughter rollicked through him.

Cabe inhaled a draft of crisp evening air. For a moment there he thought he saw the child Laura and the woman Laura all mixed together. Disconcerted by his urge to catch her in his arms, perhaps even taste that curving mouth before letting her go, he wound an escaping curl around his finger, then slowly released it.

"How about Three Oaks?"

"Three Oaks?" Laura repeated calmly when she'd have liked to squeal like a teenager. "But isn't that a private club?"

"True, but Juliet inherited her grandfather's membership, so I have guest privileges. I don't know how romantic it is," he said teasingly, "but I do know it's fancy duds and gourmet food. It's just a little after five now, so we have ample time to make our eight o'clock reservation."

"You've already made reservations?" Brown eyes flashed. "Pretty sure of yourself there, weren't you?"

Lazily, Cabe smiled. "Fairly sure of having a dinner companion, yes. These *are* my old stomping grounds." Letting a fingertip glide down her sun-warmed arm, he inquired, "You think your new neighbor could sit down for a minute, maybe even get a drink of water? Ours won't be turned on until tomorrow."

"Yes, of course, certainly you can! Sit, drink, both, inside," she said, flustered by the rapid transition from fem-

inine pique to chagrin at her lapse of manners. *My neighbor.*
It was a challenging thought. But she loved challenges.

Heather elected to stay outside, but Cabe came in. While
she poured a glass of ice water he stood looking around her
combination living-dining room appraisingly. It was sur-
prisingly important to Laura that he liked it. Trying to see
her home through his eyes, she let her gaze drift from stan-
dard beige carpet and white walls to the couch Dolly had
covered in softest yellow, apricot and cream-striped velvet,
and the forest-green chair piped in the same colorful fabric. Two terra-cotta ducks flanked a windowsill display of
flowering African violets. On the fireplace ledge a huge
white ceramic cachepot held pink-edged apple blossoms and
the furry gray buds of pussywillow branches.

Through the open bedroom door part of a queen-size bed
and its puffy, peach and green comforter and the lacy black
scrap of gown she had slept in could be glimpsed. She saw
the dark green eyes touch upon it before flickering, with a
hint of a twinkle, to hers. Blushing, Laura poured two
glasses of ice water.

Taking his, Cabe sat down on the couch. She curled up
beside him, shoes off, her legs curved and feet tucked under. "What did I say that caused you to buy the house?" she
asked eagerly.

"That it was a good investment. The building itself
checked out structurally sound, and those extra acres..."
Cabe lost track of his thoughts as a lock of soft brown hair
slithered down her neck and nestled enticingly between her
breasts. His fingertips burned. "You were right about the
town's investment potential," he started over. "With the
kind of money this area is beginning to attract I think the
demand for homes like Tulioria will soon outstrip the sup-
ply. Luckily for me the Vanderhildens believed otherwise.
Oh, by the way, did you pass that realtor's test?"

"Actually, that was just an 'Introduction to Real Estate'
class, but yes, I squeaked through. Barely. I'm beginning to

suspect my path to fame and fortune doesn't lie that way,"
Laura responded wryly. "Luckily I'm taking those other
business-oriented courses." *Does he mean to sell the house
when summer's over?* "Maybe I'll find my hidden talent in
one of them, who knows!" *Well, if so, that's something else
I'll have to work on.* "At least I'll wind up with a degree.
Why aren't you using a cane?"

"The ground's too soft and my leg's feeling better." He
eased to his feet. "I'd better take Heather on back to the
Inn, get her something to eat before I give her to your aunt.
I'll come by for you around seven-thirty. We do have a dinner date, don't we?"

Laura considered it. "Well, when I compare dinner at the
Oaks to hot dogs on the beach . . . yes, we have a date," she
decided, and silently laughed at the image of herself playing the reluctant maiden when wild horses couldn't have
stopped her from going with him.

Four

——

Wrapped in a pink towel, her rosy skin giving off the scent of perfumed bath oil, Laura put down the hairdryer and fluffed out her freshly washed hair. Excitement sparkled in her eyes and lent a sultry glow to her face, while the damp terry cloth clung like a second skin to the curves and hollows of her body. What would Cabe think if he saw me right now? she wondered as she walked to her closet.

Humming, she began rifling through her collection of "fancy duds." What did someone wear to a place like Three Oaks? "Oh, for heaven's sake, Laura, you're not exactly a country bumpkin!" she poked fun at her nervousness. But she wasn't a habitué of private clubs, either.

The dress she finally chose was a raspberry silk jersey with a wrap bodice and tulip skirt. With it she wore tinted hose and shoes that were merely a few thin, black suede straps attached to three-inch heels. Her hair was caught at her nape with a black velvet comb. Cabe gave a low whistle when she opened the door to him.

Laura simply stared, robbed of speech. Cabe McClain in a white dinner jacket, his dark, wavy hair still damp from his shower, his eyes gleaming in that ruggedly handsome face, was a woman's romantic fantasy come true.

Never had Laura come up against such potent sex appeal. His dazzling voltage flashed through her, spreading downward to pool in her stomach. The urge to throw her arms around his broad shoulders and lift her mouth to his sweet smile was nearly irresistible. To say hello she had to wet her lips. His eyes darkened in instant response to the provocative gesture and sent another unsettling thrill sizzling through her.

He smelled wonderful, spicy and alluring. He held her arm protectively as they walked to the car. In the sky a misty half-moon shone. She felt all floaty and warm inside.

He was driving a different car. "A new car?" she asked, shifting around on the velvety seat until she could watch him without being obvious about it.

"No," he said. "It's a rental car. We chartered a plane, landed at that small airport just outside of town. I suppose we'll be doing a lot of that from now on. Heather will be clamoring to come down here every weekend."

"I don't see why she can't stay here now. Why make her wait?"

"I have my reasons."

Laura remained silent as his cool, quiet voice flicked her ears. In other words, Laura, it's none of your business, she thought.

Glancing at her, he went on smoothly, "There's a lot of work to be done on the house. New tiles, countertops and flooring in the kitchen, recarpeting, repainting..."

"I can help you find the people to do all that," she jumped right back in.

"I'll do most of it myself. I like working with my hands."

Despite his easy tone Laura had the impression of another door being politely shut in her face. A quick mental shrug dispatched the sting. There were too many things she

had to learn about this green-eyed man to worry about small
rejections. Remembering, with a lovely little jolt, that there
would be plenty of time for that later, she led him into
deeper discussion about his remodeling project and the
twenty minute drive passed effortlessly.

The Oaks, once a working rice plantation, was now a
country club with a nine-hole golf course and an acre of
meticulously kept lawn. The spacious dining room was well
lighted, its gold, navy and white decor crisp rather than soft.
Still, there was no question that a man dressed up in formal
clothes did feel romantic escorting a lady into such under-
stated opulence, Cabe admitted to himself. Especially when
that lady was as beguiling as the one seated across from him.

He couldn't get over the change in her. The tousled gam-
ine he had met earlier that evening had metamorphosed into
a startlingly poised sophisticate.

Sensing the reason for his bemused expression, Laura had
a quirky notion to remind him that appearances could be
deceiving. She felt about as stable as a bowl of Jell-O. This
new side of Cabe shredded even more of her comfortable,
present images. She was seeing an urbane, worldly man who
undoubtedly felt as much at ease in famed cosmopolitan
restaurants as he did here.

"I think I'll have the roast quail," he said. "What about
you?"

Laura chose a luxuriously thick, succulent veal chop,
grilled with a sprinkling of wild mushrooms, served on a
nest of tender lambs' lettuce with roasted red peppers in a
straw potato basket. It was all delicious, as was his double
dutch chocolate cheesecake and the silky caramelized cus-
tard that flowed down her throat like a breath of perfumed
air.

She ate daintily, albeit with a gusto that kept Cabe smiling and stirred up appetites that could not be appeased by
the richest dessert. Everything about her captivated him. He
could get utterly caught up in her breathy, rushing chatter.
The thick-lashed eyes that kept ensnaring his were capable

of turning solemn, mischievous, flirtatious or innocent with bewildering speed.

Their light social chatter required no effort. During the return drive, Cabe found a radio station that played ballads from the sixties, and they listened for the most part in companionable silence.

But when they were sitting in her living room enjoying a nightcap, the closeness of shared memories generated its own spontaneous intimacy. They sat an arm's length apart. His body insisted on getting closer. Leaning into the separating distance he inhaled her sweet scent, felt the sensuous warmth emanating from her ripe body. He tasted with his imagination the curving red lips that flooded his mouth with desire. Ah, Laura, I'm drowning in you and I haven't even touched you yet, he thought.

He stretched an arm across the back of the couch. "Any boyfriends?"

Laura blinked. "Several. Except they aren't boys."

"It is a demeaning term," he agreed. "Anyone serious?" She shook her head. Pleased with her answer, he glanced at the black and white photograph of Laura, her two younger cousins, and his sister that adorned the mantle. "Where are Kacie and Eve now?" he asked with an indulgent smile. "Happily settled down with husbands and kids?"

"No. Susan's the only one who managed that. Kacie's been in Florida for the past two years. After her one true love affair went sour, she went to Florida to visit her godfather and stayed to save the whales, the harbor seals, pensioned women and Lord knows what all else. Eve went to Reno to be a dancer and ended up waiting on tables. She finally met 'the perfect guy,' but..." Laura wiped her wine-splashed fingers. "To make a long story short, she found herself pregnant and him gone, so she said to hell with him and raised her little girl alone."

"Doing that takes an enormous amount of will. You think she'll ever change her mind about needing him?"

Puzzled at his sardonic tone, Laura replied evenly, "She's recently discovered where he lives, but whether she'll ever use the information, I don't know. She's had a pretty rough time, Cabe."

"Yes, I imagine she did."

His voice was soft, his smile sweet again. Letting her gaze drift to his mouth, Laura delicately licked her lips. "What happened with you and Michele?" she asked off-handedly. "We all thought you had a great marriage."

"It was good for a while." He shrugged. "Then it just fell apart."

Absently he massaged his knee. Laura's fingers curled tightly around the stemmed glass. "She must have been very unhappy, your Michele. To lose you, I mean," she ventured.

"She seems to have survived it," Cabe said, ironic. "What about you, what's your sad story?"

"A cliché, I'm afraid." Needing time to think, Laura got up to pour more wine. What emotions did Cabe's enigmatic expression mask? Her gaze tried to probe behind it, without success. He didn't want her to know what he was feeling.

With an inward sigh she walked back to the couch. Although she would dearly love to pry, his reluctance to bare intimate details not only had to be respected, but compelled her to follow suit.

She slipped off her shoes and sat down again. "Nick was handsome, charming, careless. So charmingly careless you couldn't make yourself believe that he really didn't care. To sum up, it was a bad marriage made by a twenty-year-old woman who should have known better, and an unpleasant divorce four years later."

"No children?" he asked idly.

"No…" Again Laura hesitated. Deception came hard to her. But the truth was too personal to share just yet. That she could not trust the man she had married enough to risk bearing his children diminished her somehow.

"Kids just weren't part of the plan," she said flippantly, and saw something very similar to annoyed relief flit across his face.

"Some watchdog," he laughed and stroked the little gray dog sleeping noisily between them, leaving her to suspect her imagination again.

Cabe eased to his feet as the cuckoo clock behind them struck eleven. "I'd better go pick up Heather, let Dolly get some sleep."

They stepped outside on the moon-shadowed porch. He placed a hand on the wrought-iron upright. Confederate jasmine climbed it. That's what she smelled like tonight, he realized, this heavenly scent suffusing the air all around them.

"Thank you for a lovely evening, Laura," he said softly. Without conscious intent, he tucked a silky brown lock back into its velvet comb.

"Thank you," she said.

"You're welcome," he said. Then he bent his head and kissed her.

Laura froze, still wary of the feelings he brought her, then relaxed as he made no move to alter the light press of lips. Another little do-nothing kiss, she thought, smiling as he lifted his head with a breezy "See you tomorrow."

Later, lying in bed listening to the nightly concert serenade outside her open window, Laura thought back on the stimulating interlude on her couch, talking, laughing, opening up a little more to each other, and from there to the gentle moment on her porch. Closing her eyes, she experienced again the feel of his hard, warm mouth, savored the magic in the word "tomorrow." Now don't go building dream castles around that man, she cautioned herself. But it was hard to stop dreaming. Cabe's was the kind of vibrant masculinity instantly recognized by a woman. His manner seduced rather than dominated; his quicksilver smile melted the wall between fantasy and realism. It was well into the morning before her excitement calmed to a soft longing that was not wholly of the body.

Although her sleep was fitful, Laura rose early, as usual, and went about her morning routine, which included a three-mile run on the jogging path on the road along the river. She was enjoying coffee on her patio when Heather burst around the corner shouting her name. KK leaped up to meet her. Behind Heather came Cabe, exasperation written all over his face. Clad in white drawstring pants and a clingy red T-shirt, he looked incredibly attractive. Laura let a wave suffice for a greeting. Her heart was beating so fast she felt breathless.

He scolded Heather and apologized to Laura for the intrusion.

She replied that it was the loveliest intrusion possible.

Responding to Heather's awed shout, they turned to view a small white ocean liner gliding by not a hundred yards away.

"Beautiful, isn't it," Laura said softly. "The Cape Fear River is part of the international waterway, Heather. You'll see all kinds of boats going up and down it. I've got a boat, too. Maybe you'd like to take a ride in it sometime."

Heather drew back. "No, thank you." She ran to Cabe.

"Heather had a bad experience with boats, she was on one that overturned, and it takes a while to get over that," Cabe explained quietly.

"Yes, I guess it does," Laura said, feeling awkward again. "Well! What are you two going to do today?"

"Just hang around, Daddy says," Heather answered. "I wish we could go with you instead. I like your store, it's fun. There are ghosty things in the attic," she told her father.

"My grandfather's marine collection," Laura explained.

"Sounds interesting," Cabe said. "Are you working today?"

"Yes, Saturdays are our busiest days. I'd love to hang around with you two instead, but my classes take up so much of my working time now...but I'm off tomorrow."

"I'm going to New York tomorrow." Cabe spoke more brusquely than intended. The sight of her was testing his willpower more than he had believed possible. She smelled like old-fashioned garden flowers after a rain, fresh and clean and appealing. Her hair fell soft and loose around her shoulders and she wore a long, thin terry-cloth robe over nothing but warm, golden skin.

The look of disappointment clouding her eyes ensnarled his heart in another unwanted reaction. "We do have to be on hand when those new appliances arrive. But maybe later we'll have time to stop by the store, maybe even pick up a picnic lunch to eat on our new terrace, how's that?" he asked.

"Sounds great," Laura replied. She was not unaware of the effect she was having on her handsome friend. Reluctantly she excused herself and went inside to dress for work.

Dolly met her at the door of the store. "Pearl's waiting," she said by way of greeting. Chuckling, Laura put on her pink smock and went to the back room where Pearl was stacking her latest works of art.

They were frameless, and hung easily on the fence. Pearl stepped back to admire their handiwork. "Do you think any of them will sell today? Oh, I pray they do."

Laura frowned, disquieted by her aunt's fervency. "They certainly should, Aunt Pearl, they're absolutely exquisite. You just haven't been discovered yet is all." Linking arms, they strolled back into the hubbub of a busy Saturday morning.

Traffic jammed the road to the beach and flooded the island ferry as summer people streamed in. No pictures sold, but picnic supplies and cold drinks went at a fast clip and their new frozen yogurt machine was hard put to keep up with the demand. Maybe I didn't make a mistake buying this expensive toy after all, Laura thought, her spirits rising as the stacks of cups lowered.

Cabe never came in for his picnic supplies. Laura supposed they decided to eat elsewhere. Hiding her disap-

pointment, she took advantage of the one o'clock business
lull to catch a breath of fresh air on the veranda. Pearl
brought her some of the silky peach yogurt swirled prettily
in a Styrofoam cup.

"One of the miniscapes sold," she said, avoiding Laur-
a's gaze. "Twelve dollars."

"That's great, Aunt Pearl! Twelve dollars is twelve dollars."

Pearl's answering smile was weak and oddly uncertain. "I
reckon."

Dolly materialized beside her. "Oh. Pearl. I didn't know
you were back here. The breadman wants to see you. I think
he's sweet on her, too," she sighed to Laura.

Chuckling as her aunt hurried off, Laura gave Dolly a
quizzical look. "Is something wrong, Aunt Dolly?" she
asked as the older woman fidgeted with her apron.

"Yes, something's wrong, and bad as I hate to lay more
trouble on your shoulders...it's Pearl, honey. She's talking about selling her pearls and you've got to change her
mind. She thinks because they're from her mother-in-law's
so-called estate that they're worth hundreds of dollars. But
I took them to the jeweler for her once to get the clasp fixed
and he said they weren't worth the cost of restringing. But
you can't tell a woman that about something she prizes as
an heirloom."

"No, of course you can't," Laura agreed, bewildered.
"But why on earth would she want to sell them?"

"Because she's going to need a lot of money in the next
month or so. You know she had that dental appointment.
Well, she doesn't just have a few cavities, she needs two
crowns, and then periodontal surgery—well, I'll let her tell
you about it," Dolly decided as Laura's eyes began flashing.

She left to summon Pearl, who was nearly in tears by the
time her irate niece finished chewing her out. "Laura, you
don't understand, we're talking a lot of money here even

without the surgery. Lord, if you include that it's nearly two thousand dollars! I couldn't dump all that on you!''

It was an appalling sum of money. But that's no excuse for keeping it from me, she thought angrily. I'm young and strong, I can carry the load for them. ''Aunt Pearl, have you forgotten I sold a house?''

''But that check's for taxes and bills, not for personal expenses—''

''That check is also for necessities, and dental bills certainly qualify for that. So no more nonsense about selling your precious pearls. I'm in charge now,'' Laura said with reasonably brisk competence. *And thank you, Cabe,* she thought.

He came in around three, on his way to the airport. Pearl had had a date the previous night and missed meeting Heather. ''Well, if you aren't just the sweetest thing!'' she enthused. Ignoring Dolly's rather smug introduction, she leaned to the little girl's level and held out her hand. ''Hi there, I'm Laura's Aunt Pearl.''

''Hi.'' Solemn green eyes raised to Pearl's warm gaze. ''Can I call you Aunt Pearl, too?''

''Heather,'' Cabe reproved. ''You may call her Mrs. Stewart.''

''Why, Cabe, surely you wouldn't deprive me of the joy of being called aunt by this adorable child?'' Pearl said, looking terribly deprived.

''Pitiful. Just pitiful,'' Dolly opined, hands on hips and glaring at Pearl's quivering-lip act. Cabe and Laura burst out laughing. But his eyes betrayed a trace of annoyance.

Agreeing, amiably, that he could deny her nothing, Cabe said his goodbyes and started to leave, only to confront the group of spirited senior citizens who had just walked in. They were all long-time acquaintances of Laura's grandmother and weren't in the least shy about displaying their interest in him.

Laura didn't interfere; she wanted to test him. Or rather she wanted to test the polished, charmingly arrogant male

she had met last night over a restaurant dinner table. That
man would have no patience with a bunch of eccentric old
ladies. With unswerving intent, she introduced him, and
permitted each to trap them both for a measured moment.

It had been an important test. Feeling a little giddy with
relief, she finally extracted Cabe from his circle of admirers
and took him and Heather out the back door. While his
child scrambled onto the glider, he moved Laura to the railing for a private word. "Don't look so innocent, I know
what you did to me in there," he growled.

"But I did nothing," she protested, turning her laughing, dark eyes on his face.

"The devil you did nothing. You're always doing something—" Breaking off, he glanced at Heather.

"All right, I did," Laura conceded, "But I wanted to see
how you'd react to a sensitive but annoying situation."

"I see," Cabe said. "No, I don't. How *should* I have reacted?"

"Exactly as you did," she said in her softest voice.

Tuesday evening Laura found an envelope slipped under
her front door. It contained a check and a very nice letter
from the Vanderhildens. Laura appreciated their senti-
ments, but the check was a letdown. "Not even enough to
take care of Pearl's surgery," she muttered. Well, the aunts
need not know that. Nor Cabe either, her pride spoke up.
She dismissed Cabe. He was too much on her mind lately.

As countless other women could probably have told her,
Laura thought dryly, dismissing Cabe was easier said than
done. An odd sense of breathlessness assailed her every time
she remembered he'd be back in two days—to stay.

He had left her the extra key to the house, and the cold
snap that rode in on fierce winds and rain Thursday morning provided her with what she thought was a perfect way to
welcome him home. What he would actually think was good
for an extra shiver as she parked in his drive that evening.

As she suspected, the house was unpleasantly dark and chilly. She turned on lights, the furnace, the intercom-radio. In no time at all music and warmth swirled through the echoing rooms. An oak and applewood fire crackled cheerfully in the fireplace. Yellow jonquils in a square glass vase graced the hearth. Candles flickered.

Two rattan chairs and a small table made do for furniture. She centered them in front of the fireplace, then went to the kitchen. Soon the fragrance of coffee and apple strudel spiced the air.

Hearing a car pull in, Laura positioned herself in front of a second-story window that overlooked the driveway. Her heart began its skipping beat as she watched Cabe get out of the car and stand gazing up at her. The light from a tall pole-lamp shot glints through his damp, dark hair and glittered in his eyes. He closed the car door and was lost from view.

When he entered the house Laura let out a tremulous breath. The twinges of panic constricting her chest made breathing almost painful. If this reaction was any indication, having Cabe McClain for a neighbor could be more of a challenge than she had bargained for.

Five

Laura met him at the top of the stairs. "Hi," she said with a trace of uncertainty. Would he resent what she'd done?

"Laura..." Setting down the shopping bag he toted, Cabe took it all in with one swift glance. "This is a surprise! I was expecting a dark, empty house and instead I find lights, fresh flowers, a fire..." He glanced at the brown sugar and cinnamon-glazed strudel. "Is that homemade?"

"From the bakery, but you'll love it," Laura decreed. Pleasure and relief flowed through her voice. "Here, let me take your jacket. Is Heather coming again this weekend?"

"No. She couldn't miss her class slumber-party even for me," he said, chuckling.

"Slumber parties are very important to girls," she assured him gravely. "Why no cane again?"

"Doc said to use it at my own discretion from now on," he said. Tossing his jacket over an empty box, he glanced at her. "Laura, seems to me you've gone to a lot of trouble here—"

"Oh, nonsense, no trouble at all," Laura shushed him crisply, but compassion tremored her voice. His light, firm posture gave the impression of standing without effort. His tall, straight figure in the single gray of slacks and shirt lent his body the look of being poised for action on an instant's notice—and then that misgaited step.

Swallowing, Laura indulged her fingers by brushing a few raindrops from his hair, then bade him sit while she poured coffee and served the strudel.

"Is it good?" she asked as he bit into the sweet cake.

Cabe's gaze raced over the rose-colored mohair sweater she wore. Her long hair caught in its deep, cowl collar, and the glowing hue illumined her satiny skin. "It's good," he said gruffly.

Laura curled up in the other chair and arranged her cream woolen skirt around her shapely legs. Sitting before the fire enjoying their small repast, they discussed many things, none of them more than superficially personal, before falling into a silence that nurtured the vibrant sense of intimacy. Watching the play of firelight on his rugged face, she wondered what he was thinking, feeling. She had never seen anyone more inscrutable than Cabe McClain.

Cabe's mask only extended so far. His eyes, disobedient to the commands of his brain, had fixed on her rosy mouth. He was too absorbed with mentally tracing the sharp, full peaks of her upper lip with the tip of his tongue, to immediately realize she was speaking. "What?" he asked blankly.

Amused, she replied, "I said tell me about Brazil."

Liking the way she hung on to his every word, Cabe told her of orchids spilling through Amazonian foliage, brilliant birds like flickers of flame in a dense green canopy, and rainbows arching over mist-sheathed waterfalls; of Bahia and its watercolor buildings, Rio and its smiling, sexy Cariocas, the sugar white sands of Copacabana.

"What I wouldn't give to see all that!" Laura sighed. Her eyes narrowed. "I suppose you met the prototypes of the famous 'Girl from Ipanema'? What were they like?"

Crossing his hands behind his neck, Cabe smiled lazily. "All tanned and gorgeous, all clad in the latest version of the bikini: a strategic patch and a few pieces of string they call the *tanga*. The beaches aren't bad, either. I plan to adopt some of their more practical ideas for my own use. Like decking the hot tub I plan to have installed in the swirling patterns of Rio's famous black-and-white mosaic seaside sidewalk."

"I can recommend someone for the job," Laura said.

Cabe frowned, his good feeling vanishing as she went on. She had made a list of reputable businesses for him. Newspaper service began tomorrow, she said, wriggling slender feet back into her shiny pumps. There were breakfast foods and more coffee in the kitchen. Tomorrow was her day off, and she was free to help him do such things as go to the supermarket to stock that gorgeous new refrigerator and walk-in pantry. Then she would take him to meet a friend who was an expert at making and hanging draperies.

Cabe roughed a hand through his hair. Naturally he was flattered at the trouble she'd gone to for him. Actually he'd felt ten foot tall when he'd walked in and found her waiting. But she was taking too much for granted!

Rising, he cleared his throat, and prepared to speak to her in the reasoning tone he'd used when she was a little girl. But it wasn't a little girl who looked up at him. It was a desirable woman.

His hands clenched and unclenched as she leaned over to clear the table. It was incredible how soft and touchable she looked in that pretty outfit.

But he couldn't touch. So he spoke irritably.

"Laura, leave the clean-up, you've already done too much now. That includes tomorrow, too. I appreciate your offer, but you don't have to waste your day off herding me around town. Or wear yourself out running back and forth over here, for that matter. I'm quite capable of buying food and drapes without someone holding my hand."

She put down the tray and slowly straightened to face him. "I know that, Cabe. But I don't consider it too much, you'd do the same for me if the situation was reversed. But if you think I've over-stepped my bounds..." She let it trail off, a dimple flickering tenuously.

"Laura," Cabe half groaned, accepting his defeat. "You have no intention of letting me get on alone, do you."

"None."

Her gaze was completely guileless. In spite of himself, a laugh rumbled in Cabe's chest.

"I guess that's put plainly enough," he said, his grin so lopsided that Laura had to hug him.

The spontaneous gesture brought her breasts against his shirtfront and aligned her belly and thighs to taut-muscled masculinity. Laura sucked in her breath as desire spiraled through her, quick and hot and strong. Without hesitation she slid her fingers through his thick hair and leaned into his unyielding contours.

As if compelled, his arms shot around her. She quivered, anticipating his masterful touch. But the hands he balled into fists rested rigidly on the small of her back. She felt him tremble as her lips feathered along the bronzed column of his neck. His body heat fused with hers, making Laura flamingly aware of how much she wanted this closeness. She wanted to kiss and be kissed, touch and be touched, and then...

Leaving it there for the time being, she concentrated on the mesmerizing warmth that flowed through her. It affected every part of her body. Her toes tingled. Her legs were velvet. Her thighs ached for the heat of friction and her breasts kindled. He shifted stance and hard male flesh pressed deep into feminine softness. An erotic shiver flashed along the entire length of her form. Letting her head fall back, she lowered her lashes to the level of his mouth, then raised the lacy fans to meet his gaze, her eyes slightly slanted, a low, smoky laugh parting her lips.

The bewitchery of that look provoked Cabe to a muttered oath. He had gone painfully tense, his heart slamming out a wild new beat as he found himself with his arms full of Laura. He had managed to keep his head, but his defensive shifting tactic had dangerously backfired. Knowing there was no way he could force his arms to let go of her yet, he had tried to curb his blazing response by blocking her seductive softness with a neutral part of his body. But she had shifted with him and somehow they were snugged closer than ever.

She felt meltingly pliant, deliciously female to his vibrating male senses. All the things he wanted to do to her shot through his mind with sizzling clarity. Off limits! he reminded himself harshly. She ran her tongue over her lips and his mouth heated. He had never in his life needed to kiss a woman like he needed to kiss this one. When her parted lips came close enough to touch with his tongue, his mouth simply dipped down and took what it wanted.

Cabe fought to keep the kiss superficial. To no avail; he could not prevent himself from tasting the sweetness that lay beyond the twin peaks of her lips. His greedy tongue explored every honeyed surface and hollow before he pulled back.

When he finally lifted his head, she reacted with a gaspy catch of breath. She didn't make it any easier and clung to him.

Her hair nuzzled his chin and he took refuge there until the earthquakes going on inside him ran their courses. Baffled and angered by the intensity of his desire, he told himself it wouldn't last long. All he need do was keep a tight rein on his baser nature when he was alone with her, and sooner or later this electrifying attraction would dissipate. Then he could enjoy the allure of her without being sucked into a whirlpool, Cabe concluded with bone-dry humor.

Putting some space between them, he eased his resistive hands to her shoulders. An uneven smile tugged at her lips as she looked up at him. He ruffled her hair. "I think we have a problem, Laura."

Candid brown eyes met his gaze squarely. "Not *we*, Cabe. I have no argument with what just happened," she replied, disconcertingly direct.

"All right, then I have a problem."

"With what?"

"With you," he said, chuckling. "I keep looking for a girl and finding a troublesome seductress. You've grown into quite a terrifying woman, Laura, all that siren power. Sets a mere, ordinary man to shaking in his boots."

Assessing the strain in his teasing tone, Laura felt a giddy taste of that power. With a soft laugh she brushed her knuckles across his mouth. "You're not an ordinary man, Cabe," she murmured.

"No, that I'm not," he said mildly. "I'll have to stop forgetting that." Rousing himself, he glanced at his watch. "It's been a long day and looks to be an even longer one tomorrow," he remarked, yawning.

"Yes, it is getting late," Laura agreed dryly. "Almost nine o'clock." Fishing his key from her skirt pocket, she laid it on the table. "When is your furniture arriving? Saturday?"

"A few pieces ordered locally will be delivered tomorrow, but the rest arrives Saturday."

"I don't envy you. Moving is the pits." Laura grabbed her shawl from the banister and swung down the stairs. She didn't mind her wild flux of emotions, but she didn't want him seeing it. "Don't come down, Cabe, I'll lock the door behind me. Good night," she called and went out without a backward glance.

KK was waiting at the cottage window, delirious with happiness at her homecoming. Dodging his frantic kisses, Laura put him outside for his nightly run and began tidying up the kitchen. She was still caught up in Cabe's spell and her actions were automatic. A shiver danced down her spine as she relived the drugging delight of his hard mouth

taking hers in a deep, hungry kiss. How far would it have
gone had he not broken it off? And why had he? Out of
concern for her, she supposed. In her present mood she
couldn't decide whether to appreciate that or resent it.

The issue was still unsettled when she finally slid into bed.
Seldom did she sleep nude, but tonight the cool, silky sheets
felt good against her overly warm body. She felt good, too,
all achy and wanting. She had told Cabe the truth; she had
no problems with the passion that had exploded between
them. Why on earth should she? To feel every fiber of her
body come alive, every nerve tingle with that special excitement, was a glorious experience. Just imagining his big
hands seeking out her womanly secrets sent a long,sinuous
shiver down her lower torso.

She closed her eyes and pictured him intimately. Her
erotic thoughts, like her approach to life, were unabashedly
frank and direct. When she envisioned his lean, bronzed
body stretched out beside her, there was nothing between
them but air.

How would Cabe react if he knew she was lying here enjoying such blunt sexual thoughts? Probably go into shock,
she thought puckishly. Flopping onto her stomach, she
curled her arms around her pillow and drifted into a fantasy that would have reddened his ears.

Just before Laura fell asleep, a displeasing, will-o'-the-
wisp thought drifted across her mind. It gained considerably more substance in bright morning sunlight. She had not
forgotten his rough-edged protest the night before and although she tried, she could not shake the suspicion that he
might consider her something of a nuisance.

Don't go imagining things, she advised herself. The possibility's way too slim to take seriously. But just on the off
chance that I was too aggressive, maybe I'd be wise to keep
to myself today, go to the library, get some studying done.
Maybe it would be best to just suspend all contact with Cabe
indefinitely, she concluded, beginning to feel the scratch on
her pride.

* * *

Laura was just completing a three-mile run Sunday morning and contemplating breakfast when she saw Pearl and Dolly descending upon Cabe with potted plants and assorted casseroles.

Cabe was on the terrace at the time. Aware that the ladies of her aunt's social club had taken it upon themselves to look after him—just until he got himself squared away, Dolly said—Laura stopped behind a hedge of wild roses to watch his reaction.

He was warm and gracious, charming them, charming her. The lean, lithe look of him in faded jeans and a sleeveless sweatshirt created a milky softness at the back of her knees. Fearing that he might think she was spying on him, which she was, Laura admonished herself to get a hold of herself and pushed through the hedge to join them.

His head tipped in a listening attitude, Cabe watched her approach, his green eyes glinting. "Laura," he said, inclining his dark head.

"Cabe," Laura said, lightly mocking his gesture. Glancing at his curving mouth, she moistened her lips and tasted him there. His expression was as unrevealing as it had been Thursday night. Had he applied the same willful denial to their passionate kiss? Or hadn't he felt it, too, the trembling inside, the pounding blood and fiery desire that left a body aching long after the moment was over? Ignoring the tightness in her chest, she greeted her aunts with the usual kiss on the cheek, then leaned back against the railing and exercised her gift of social chatter.

After the women left him in peace, Cabe squinted at the one who would not, whether in or out of view. "This is the third time this week I've been descended upon by Fair Harbor's self-appointed Welcome Wagon," he said with wry humor. "What do you expect it would take to stop, or at least slow down, this charitable deluge?"

"Cabe, you haven't a chance of escaping their good-natured concern," Laura informed him gently. "Your sit-

uation's just too appealing to feminine souls. The only way
to stop them is to hurt them, and if you did that, you'd have
me to deal with.''

"I would, hmm?" Cabe's amusement faded as chill
brown eyes leveled on his face.

"You would. I'd not be kind to someone who hurt my
aunts.''

She smiled and he saw the steel in her, and had no doubt
she meant what she said. Would she wrap her man in that
fiercely protective cloak? Did she realize that big, strong,
powerful hulks like himself could be as fragile as a child at
times?

He shoved at his hair. "Laura, believe it or not, I don't
get my kicks hurting people. But I do believe in saying what
I think. Look, about that incident Thursday night—"

"You mean when I put my arms around you and came
close to you.''

"Er, yes—"

"And you kissed me and held me even closer.''

Cabe expelled a silent oath at his body's kindling response. It was as if he were a puppet and his muscles the
drawstrings she pulled at will. Raising her arms to secure the
dusky cloud of hair beneath its banded scarf, she presented
him with a desirable picture. She wore brief white running
shorts and a sleeveless blouse tied at her midriff.

"I mean when our natural affection for one another took
a wrong turn," he snapped, his anger flaring as enchanting
dark eyes jerked the strings tighter. How could she entice
him one second and infuriate him the next?

"I don't agree with that," she fired back. She spared his
face a glance, her amused curl of lip sending his temper
soaring as her defiance gave way to indulgence. "But out of
concern for your blood pressure, I'll hush up and let you tell
me what you want from me. Or don't want, whatever.''

"What I *want*," he said, maddened at what he wanted,
"is for you to stop what you're doing or trying to do—
whatever—to me." He caught her soft shoulders. "What I

want is to keep intimacy out of our friendship. I don't need that kind of trouble and neither do you. I also don't need all this neighborly concern, good-hearted as it undoubtedly is—"

She winced at his tight grip, vastly enriching Cabe's burden. His frustration boiled over in a furious burst of sound. "And I most certainly don't need you and that seductive body and that sexy laugh to keep me awake at night!"

Laura tried to speak, but couldn't. Cabe flung his hands from her and clenched them at his sides. He looked as stunned as she felt, she thought. Her mind whirled. Which took precedence, her blazing resentment, or the thrill of his provocative remark? One canceled out the other, leaving her comically confused.

Recovering, she gave a brittle laugh and placed a finger across his angry mouth. "In a nutshell, you want me to stop being a nuisance and to keep my distance. So okay. No more impositions, friend Cabe, neighborly or otherwise. There. Now you can sleep at night."

"Laura—"

Cutting him off, she wheeled around and resumed her jogging, letting a wriggle of fingers over one shoulder suffice for a farewell.

Although he had to physically restrain himself, Cabe didn't go after her. No reason to, he thought briskly. When you got right down to it, she'd said everything he wanted to say—in a nutshell.

That afternoon he saw her at the top of an old apple tree gathering flowering branches. He thought about assisting her. At least give her the devil for taking such risks with herself, he reflected, tempted to grab the opportunity to vent more of his churning frustration. But the set of her chin suggested he think twice about that. Instead he went down to the hardware store and bought a bicycle.

Despite his long, therapeutic ride, by evening he felt so restless his muscles creaked. Friend Cabe, he admonished himself sardonically, you've been too long without a woman.

The new week crawled. Four days without Laura in them had him missing her absurdly much. He missed her cheeky grin, her husky voice, her dark eyes. He longed to hear her chatter, chastise, peal off the melodious laugh that spread warmth all through him. He longed, period.

The only time he saw her was coming or going, flying across the lawn to her boat, barreling down the street in her station wagon. He'd call out or honk the horn and she would smile or flip him a cheery wave before hurrying on. It wasn't enough.

It is enough, Cabe told himself harshly. I'm getting exactly what I wanted. Peace and solitude. Needing nothing or no one. No disappointments, no explaining vague, irrational fears that I can't even explain to myself, much less a captivating woman. Let it be.

Unable to resist, he glanced across the lawn. Golden fingers of light straying from her windows beckoned invitingly. You have nothing to offer a woman like her, he reminded himself. Not so. There's companionship, laughter, sharing. That's enough, isn't it? *Not with her.* "Oh hell," Cabe muttered furiously. Fed up with his self-arguments, he got into his car and drove downtown.

A short time later he was rapping on her door. When it opened, her pleasant smile caused his knees to sag with relief.

"Hi, Cabe," she said, gravel voiced, and all his polished charm deserted him on the instant. "What's all this?" she asked, peering at him over the mass of flowers he had just thrust into her arms.

"A peace offering. Laura, we've got to talk," he said abruptly.

But Cabe didn't feel like talking. He felt like making love. To Laura. Only to Laura, he conceded painfully. When she partially turned to chide her noisy pet, the potent allure of her snatched his breath away. The pin-striped corduroy slacks she wore sported red-trimmed pockets over each enticing mound of her backside. A soft, white blouse molded her breasts and bared her slim, elegant throat. He would start there, press his lips to that tiny hollow and feel the life pulsing there, follow her honeyed warmth downward, and wet the thin white fabric around her nipples until they glowed through it, wine pink and erect...

Her judging silence jolted him back to reality. His head spun as he met her grave dark eyes; words dried in his mouth. She stood there, holding her flowers and looking so lovely his chest constricted. Impossibly, she was both aloof and alluring. In the soft lamplight the wealth of sun-brown hair spilling down her back shimmered and moved captivatingly. Suddenly he wanted nothing more than to take her in his arms and guard her against the world.

Struggling with his embattled self, Cabe was ill-prepared for the uncertainty that stole in to nip at his ego. Wasn't she going to ask him in?

Without speaking, she drifted away from the door, adding a sizzling streak of resentment to his ferment. His green eyes smoldering, Cabe trailed after her. He didn't consciously step inside. He simply followed the red-trimmed pockets.

Six

Smiling, Laura motioned Cabe to a chair while she drew the long breath needed to calm her erratic heartbeat. She wanted to end their estrangement. She was basically an optimist and she didn't hold grudges, they required too much energy to maintain. But her stubborn pride wouldn't permit conciliatory gestures. So she had gone about her business and quietly ached. Now joy ran wild and unruly in her veins, but she was wary.

"What did you want to talk about, Cabe?" she prompted as he tensely sat down.

"About where I've gone wrong trying to establish a workable relationship," Cabe said with deep-throated huskiness. "Laura, I'm sorry I lost my head and blew up at you—I don't even know why I did it. Maybe because I'm having a devil of a time trying to find a slot to fit you into. Any category I devise for you self-destructs the minute we get together.

"Everything seems to be a mess, including our friendship. I want us back to normal. I want you running in and out of my house like it belonged to you—"

"I never did that!"

"Yes, you did. And I've been going a little crazy these past few days—" He paused, an eyebrow lifting at her pleased smile. "So can we for God's sake just sit down together like two sensible adults and hammer out our differences?"

"I'm all for that," Laura said, sinking down on the couch.

"Me, too. But I'm not much good at expressing my feelings, especially when they're feelings I shouldn't be having." He paused, seeking words.

"You're attracted to me," she said matter-of-factly. "And you don't like it."

"Laura, it's not a matter of liking—"

"Because you're afraid you'll wake up one morning in my bed and find me in your shirt making coffee," she continued as if he hadn't spoken. She sighed. "I'm sorry, I should have worded that better. I know I can be too outspoken sometimes."

"You couldn't have worded it better; that's exactly what's got me so worried."

Her gaze didn't waver. "Why? What bothers you about the prospect of waking up to me some morning? Are you afraid I can't handle it?"

"I have no idea whether you can or not. But I do know you're not the kind of woman a man chooses for an affair." His tone shaded to ruefulness. "At least not sensibly, since I'd like nothing better than to pick you up and carry you off to bed without a thought to the consequences."

Needing a diversion, Laura got up to put her flowers in water. His provocative remark was a good sign, she thought. Establishing a comfortable relationship would be a great deal easier if the electricity thrumming between them was considered just a natural part of it.

"What consequences?" she tossed over her shoulder. "You think Pearl and Dolly would come after you with shotguns?"

Cabe chuckled. He was enjoying their intimate give and take almost as much as he would enjoy carrying out his caveman urges. "I wouldn't rule out the possibility entirely," he mused. "But you know and I know that kind of involvement would open up a whole nest of snakes."

"Well Cabe, that's certainly a nice choice of words!" she protested. "Snakes. Ugh."

"Sorry. Complications, then. Can you imagine what it would be like living this close to each other if it went sour between us?"

"I have a pretty good imagination."

"Yeah, same here," Cabe muttered, watching the red-trimmed pockets move about the kitchen. He joined her at the sink, thrusting blossoms into the vase until she slapped his hands. Scowling, he jammed them in his back pockets. Playfulness. He loved it.

She laughed softly. "Cabe, you didn't ask, but this is what *I* want, for us to be able to talk and act like this. No walking on eggshells or having to watch every word we say, just feeling free to be natural with each other."

"I'm in total agreement," he declared.

"Are you?" She looked up at him. "I'm very attracted to you."

He dug his hands deeper into his pockets. "The feeling is mutual, Laura, you know that. But we don't have to act on it. We're steadfast friends, genuinely fond of each other. I see no reason why we can't just relax and enjoy what we have without muddling it up with sex."

Laura turned aside, her lips curving in tender amusement. "We can try, Cabe," she murmured.

Laura loved storms. They made her feel eager and restless. The storm that came ashore just at sunset the next evening was in the form of a dense, blue-black blanket shot through with jagged streaks of lightning. It was made-to-order for the soft laughter and liquid murmurings of the bedroom. Chiding her erotic flight of fancy, she called KK inside and closed the door.

The small dog shook off a miniature shower of raindrops and shivered pitifully. "Oh, baby, come here," she murmured. After covering him with his favorite afghan, she sat down at her grandmother's antique writing desk to post the checks written earlier that day.

One was for Pearl's lengthy afternoon dental session. Laura sighed as she thought ahead to her aunt's scheduled surgery. *Less than two weeks from now*, she reminded herself glumly. *And I still haven't figured out how I'm going to come up with the money.* She lifted her chin defiantly. *I'll think of something.*

What she thought of was how wonderful it would be to grab a bottle of wine and dash over to Cabe's, sit in those old rattan chairs in front of the fire and share the elemental excitement of the storm. Her prickly pride rejected the tempting idea. She would return to his house only on express invitation.

When it came later that week, Laura was dressing for a dance she had little desire to attend. The sound of Cabe's deep voice made her sink down on her bed. "I'm a bit rushed for time, but I suppose I can run over for a minute or two," she answered his brief request.

The nonchalance she affected was fabulously fake. Walking through the balmy gold and blue evening, her mood alternated between eagerness and an urge to take his head off the instant she saw him.

Cabe was waiting on the terrace, tall and infinitely attractive in dark blue warm-ups. Her heart was thumping before she completed the steps. "What did you want to show me?" she asked impatiently.

He chuckled and bowed her into the den. The beautifully furnished room stopped Laura in her tracks. The worn tile floor and shabby chairs had vanished. She stood ankle-deep in plush carpet, gazing at pale, silky leather couches and Plexiglas tables with swirling copper bases. A cozy fireplace arrangement featured two lily-print wing chairs perfect for pulling up to a cheery winter fire. His collection of sculpture and wall art would do justice to a museum, she thought. She hadn't even known he was a collector.

"I thought you said the place was a mess?"

Cabe eyed her cautiously. Her gaze was chilly when it tangled with his, her manner distant.

"A couple of days ago it was, but you weren't interested despite the fact that I practically begged," he growled. "I hired Ingrid Hall to bring quick order out of chaos."

Laura didn't need to be told that, she had seen the woman flitting in and out of his house. "I'd hardly call a passing mention 'begging,'" she returned coolly. "I've been a little swamped myself lately. I spent most of yesterday with Aunt Pearl and skipped classes so Dolly could stay with her today."

"Pearl's ill?"

"She had several cavities filled yesterday and two temporary crowns put in this morning. Pearl's nerves aren't too strong," Laura defended her aunt's childish terror of dentists. "Who's Ingrid Hall?" she asked, trying to conceal her antagonism to the name.

She didn't succeed. He tipped back his head and grinned. "An old acquaintance I saw again a week or so ago. I'm letting her do something she calls Room Design for me."

"Oh?" Careless dark eyes glanced off his face. "What else does she do for you?"

The provocative question came out of that flower-like face with preposterous innocence. Enjoying it, he let his gaze roam over his alluring visitor. She had on her sexy red pumps again. A white satin blouse clung ardently to the points of her breasts. The neckline ties were left undone and a wisp of creamy lace tantalized his male senses.

Desire stirred, and his fingers curled. Both annoyed and forcibly amused by the urge to grab that gripped him every time he got too close to Laura, Cabe decided to ignore her impertinent question. Then, remembering she had a date that evening, the second one that week, in fact, he let a taunt creep into his grin.

"None of your business, Sunshine, but she is cooking me dinner tonight," he said, mussing the thick, soft mass of curls with a kind of savage pleasure.

Laura pulled away and smoothed her hair. We're acting like feuding lovers, she mused. It wasn't an unpleasant thought. She put a trace of hauteur into her demeanor. "I was merely curious, Cabe." And jealous, she added silently.

"Nosy, you mean."

She gave him a pained look. "Curious, I meant. I was referring to the furniture. Did she choose it?"

"No, this is all my stuff," Cabe replied. "She just put it in order."

Her voice was prim and cool. "You have very good taste."

"Thank you," Cabe said dryly.

Oh, that crooked grin! Laura thought. "I'd best be going. Walk me to the terrace? I don't think you're limping as badly now," she mused as they traversed the short distance. "Have you found a physical therapist yet?"

"Yes." Cabe let the door swing shut behind them with a sharp thud. "Laura, are you mad at me about something?" he asked abruptly. She looked surprised and assured him she was not. "Then why did it take a telephone call to get you over here?"

"Because I don't enjoy feeling like a nuisance, Cabe. Now if you'll excuse me, Jason will be here soon and he doesn't like to be kept waiting."

Jason. Cabe stared at her while the emotions rampaging just beneath the surface swirled into maddening confusion. The only one he could distinguish clearly was a swamping desire that was heavily etched with anger. The wind caught at her hair and blew it across her face. He wanted to dive into the curly mass, wallow in its softness. He vibrated with the desire to capture that tempting red mouth and plunder its delicious mystery. And he would break *Jason's* head if *Jason* so much as laid a finger on her.

Cabe's slow shake of head acknowledged his inconsistencies. Up until now his conviction that his extraordinary fondness for her stemmed from their prior acquaintance had filled him with tender resolve and a satisfying sense of honor. But it was starting to wear dangerously thin.

Casually he draped an arm over her shoulders. "Let's settle that nuisance thing once and for all, shall we? You are not now, nor have you ever been, a nuisance. You got that?" She nodded, a smile tugging at her lips. "Good. Because I need to ask a favor."

Her eyes rounded. "You, needing a favor?"

"Yes, me, needing a favor," he mimicked. "Juliet and Cord Hunter are coming in tomorrow afternoon. Heather, too, of course. The favor I need is a hostess for the dinner I'm giving that evening."

"You want me to be your hostess?"

"Yes. Of a thousand women, I'd want you."

His jesting tone didn't quite ring true to Laura. Her smile tremulous, she touched his arm. "I'd be honored, Cabe."

The next morning they met on the jogging path. He was walking. She was finishing a quick run before heading for the store. "I used to be a jogger," he mused, his gaze running over her knit shirt and brief red shorts. "I really miss it." He patted his flat belly. "Miss its benefits, too. Now that my appetite's returned, I'll be getting flabby in no time."

Laura fell into step beside him. "Biking's just as good. And there are exercise machines to take care of flab."

"I was a damn good tennis player, too. And skier."

"There are still lots of sports you can do, bowl, fish, sail, swim," she said, ignoring his brooding look. "Tennis, too, eventually. And I wouldn't rule out skiing. People with one leg ski."

Cabe frowned. "You're a pain, you know that? Every time I work up a good head of pity, you puncture it."

She broke into a little jog around him. "I suppose Michele would have indulged you?"

"No, Michele wasn't the indulgent sort. Run on ahead if you want. I'm enjoying the view tremendously."

They had reached the perimeter of his lawn. Stopping, Laura pulled off her headband and shook out her hair. "You're a lascivious man, but since you can't do anything about it in your broken down condition, I'll overlook it. You were home early last night," she observed.

"So were you."

"Well, I was tired." Laura looked at him and her breathing grew shallow. From beneath a midriff-length T-shirt his trim torso flowed beautifully into navy-blue shorts. The dark hair dusting his tanned legs did not conceal the thin, branched scar that ran from his knee to his ankle.

It was a visible legacy of his accident. A shiver skidded down her spine as Laura experienced a sudden vision of that burnished gold body lying broken and still on some jungle floor.

Shaken, she asked, "How are you doing with your party preparations? We don't get real busy at the store until around noon, so I'm free for a little while. What about food? And a baby-sitter? When are they arriving?"

"The food's being catered. They're arriving at five, with nursemaid in tow," Cabe ticked off. "I do need to clear out another bedroom for her, though."

Laura nodded. "We'll do that right after we get you a gardener," she said busily.

"I've already contacted a lawn service."

"You don't need a lawn service, you need a gardener and handyman, and you need him today," she asserted. "Luckily I happen to know one—"

"Of course you do."

Blushing, Laura scowled at him. We're making verbal love, she thought as his laughing green eyes suffused her with warmth. She stretched up on tiptoe and kissed his chin. "Oh, hush. He's a fine man and he's worked here before so he's familiar with everything already. I took the liberty of asking him about this and he was eager to be of service," she said, gauging Cabe's reaction as she spoke.

He just smiled and shook his head wonderingly. Releasing her breath, she wound up, "He doesn't have a telephone but he'll be around town. Meet me at the pier in fifteen minutes and I'll take you to him…if you don't mind a boat ride?"

Cabe didn't mind. A short time later, sitting beside her as they skimmed over the water, he thought back to the first time he'd seen her driving this vessel. His mind went from there to the reunion in her store, and then, to the memory of her holding the baby, a picture so poignant his heart contracted.

A welter of suppressed questions shot to the surface of his mind. Was she really as indifferent to having children as she let on? Why did he just want so damnably much to believe that? The last question struck him like an unexpected dart of pain; could she care for a man who might not be able to give her those children?

Angrily, he thrust aside the disturbing line of thought. Since there was absolutely no chance they'd wind up together, the whole question was moot.

Cabe gazed out across the sea, his expression somber. But he couldn't maintain his brown study. Laura chattered all the way to the store.

Pearl was there, feeling much better, she said. Dolly, beaming at her pink-cheeked niece, queried, "I thought you were taking the morning off, honey?"

"I am, but I wanted Cabe to meet someone. Here he is now," Laura said as a tall, white-haired man with alert gray eyes ambled in. "Cabe, meet your new gardener and handyman, John Ed Sweeting."

The two men shook hands and John Ed expressed his gratitude for the job, which he would begin immediately.

Then he extracted a small sack from his Windbreaker pocket and gave it to Dolly. "Found them embroidery needles you been wanting down to Southport," he said gruffly.

"Oh, John Ed, you sweet thing!" Dolly exclaimed.

"This is why John Ed's known around town as Sweet Thing," Laura confided to Cabe in a whispered aside.

The boat wouldn't start when they returned to it. "John Ed will look at it later," she said.

"Sweet Thing fixes boats, too?" Cabe queried, and nearly got his head snapped off.

"For me, he does—and don't you dare embarrass him by calling him that to his face!"

"He's under your umbrella of protection, too?"

"Yes, he is, and with good reason. You wait here, I'll run and get the station wagon."

Cabe nodded agreeably. He made himself a bet while he waited, and won it as soon as they were underway again. She picked up right where she left off.

"John Ed's been Aunt Dolly's beau for years—one of these days I'm sure they'll be married . . . soon as I can figure out a way they can afford it," she mused. "He's retired, lives by doing odd jobs now, and Aunt Dolly sure isn't getting rich off what I can pay her. But if he had a good paying position as an estate-gardener and handyman . . . Aunt Dolly wouldn't leave Pearl and the store in the lurch, though, not unless she felt she was needed elsewhere. Like if she was, say, housekeeper and child-care person on the same estate—"

"Laura, for God's sake!" Cabe protested, exasperated as she spun her merry webs around him with presumptuous insouciance. "I am right in assuming the estate you refer to is mine?"

"Well, yes—but what's wrong with that? You've got an acre of landscaped parkland to keep up. Dolly loves to cook and keep house, she adores children, and you'll need someone when Heather comes to stay for good."

"The gardener I'll give you, but Heather's my concern," Cabe said flatly. "She'll be attending a nursery school during the day and I'll be here at night. I'm an adequate cook, and daily maid service can take care of the rest."

"You mean Heather will just be getting out of one nursery school and you plan to stick her right back in another one? That's ridiculous, Cabe!"

"It's not ridiculous, it's practical," he said, wincing as she whipped into his driveway and missed his mailbox by inches. "It's also none of your business, so let's drop it, shall we?"

"What about Michele?"

Cabe caught the hand-brace. "What the hell," he asked evenly, "has Michele got to do with this?"

"Why, I—I just thought . . ." Laura stole a glance at his set face and became even more flustered. "Well, doesn't she have something to say about raising Heather?"

"She has nothing to say about raising Heather. And I do not care," he said, pronouncing each word precisely, "to discuss either my daughter's upbringing or my ex-wife with you."

His tone sliced deep. Silenced, Laura stopped beside John Ed's pickup and cut the engine. Cabe sat in profile, his jaw stiff. She had thought her question natural enough. What have I stirred up now? she wondered. And how much longer could she overlook his reaction to anything pertaining to his former wife? Just mentioning Michèle produced a change in him, sometimes sharp, like now, sometimes subtle, but always noticeable.

Gripped with unease, she rationalized by recalling her own long, painful recovery from the wounding insult of divorce and her initial aversion to even the sound of Nick's name.

"I'm not going to apologize for speaking my mind, Cabe," she said quietly. "But I am sorry if my take-charge attitude rubbed you the wrong way. I guess I've just gotten too used to handling things, of figuring out what's best and then acting on it, not because I particularly liked it, not at first, I mean, but because it was necessary. When my mother-in-law passed on, my husband was left with two young sisters to care for, and he wasn't too responsible a man.''

"So he dumped it all on your shoulders." Cabe got out of the car, his green eyes flinty. "And Dolly and Pearl—the store, John Ed, all your responsibility, too?''

"Yes," Laura said, matter-of-factly. Wondering why that should irritate him, she preceded him inside the foyer. "Anyway, I'll try to be less of a meddler in the future. Less mouthy, too,'' she added wryly. "Is it a downstairs bed-room we're cleaning?''

"Yes.'' Catching hold of her arm, he turned her to face him. "Laura, I don't want you less mouthy. And I don't want you apologizing for speaking your mind, ever.''

"Even when it hits a sore spot?''

The hurt clouding her dark eyes hit Cabe like a fist to the gut, roughening his voice even more. "Maybe that's what a sore spot needs now and then.'' Her smile was still wary, a little uncertain. "Ah, Laura,'' he half-whispered, and set his mouth to hers.

Cabe meant it to be a gentle kiss of apology. But her soft lips parted under his and offered him a taste of heaven while her sweet length pressed against him invitingly. Losing his hands in the glory of her hair, he let his tongue plunder paradise. Just for a moment, he told himself.

The moment lengthened. She wore a cotton jumpsuit that had thin straps that left her shoulders and half her back bare. His hands moved downward, the pads of his finger-tips digging softly into sun-warmed flesh. Wild and hot, his blood thundered in his ears.

Ardently responsive, Laura thrust her fingers into his hair, and arched into him. She was fluidly soft and he was thrillingly hard. Sensation after thrilling sensation quiv-ered through her and lodged in the delta of her thighs. She was on fire, burning for him. "Cabe," she whispered thickly into his delicious mouth. Softly she swayed against him.

Cabe went rigid. He was made of equal parts of fire and ice, his mind and body locked in desperate battle. The sound of his name sighing through kiss-reddened lips shattered his momentary paralysis. Doggedly he grasped her waist to put her from him. But those pliant, womanly hips canted again. His reaction to the sizzling friction was an urgent, angry caress down her back to the beginning flare of temptingly rounded flesh.

The urge to explore more intimate curves was incredibly strong. Desire shook him, and then outrage. He was losing control and there wasn't a doubt in his mind that he would be sorry later. So would she. The quicker she realized that, the better, he thought furiously.

Deliberately crude, he strained her against his aroused manhood. Instead of being offended as he'd hoped, she slid the palms of her hands across his temples and down his neck beneath his collar. His mind deserted him to follow the fiery path of fingertips gliding along his quivering shoulders. She wet her lips, then brushed them, warm and glistening, across his hard mouth. Realizing that he was being seduced— sweetly and expertly seduced!—was at once an absurd shock and a stunning drench of excitement. Like wildfire, it leaped from nerve to throbbing nerve as he cut short her tantalizing tease with a deep, hungry kiss.

Laura wasn't teasing, she was simply following her instincts. Far too enraptured to heed anything but her own drugging pleasure, she initiated the stimulating duel of tongues with voluptuous enjoyment. When their lips parted, they were both trembling.

The weakness only she could induce in his powerful body rendered Cabe helpless for another small eternity. The suspicion that they could end this in his bed blazed a twisted trail through his loins. Savagely he reminded himself why his code of decency had placed her off limits. Even if what he felt for her was something more complex than common lust, she deserved better than a man who could offer her only a barren cynical heart. She deserved love and commitment. He was empty of both. She deserved children....

"Laura, I'm sorry," he said. His voice roughened as he listened to the breath she drew and its slow, uneven release.

Hazy dark eyes impacted with his. "Hush. The only thing I'm sorry for is that you stopped. I love kissing you, Cabe," she said with the candid innocence that could turn him inside out.

He pushed himself away from temptation and stared at her. "What the devil am I going to do with you?" he muttered.

"Whatever feels right and natural," she said simply.

"Anything done in the heat of passion feels beautifully right and natural, Mary Laura," he drawled. "It's called the mating instinct."

Her chin came up in touching defiance. "Which can also be blindingly beautiful."

"Blinding's the right word for it, all right," he agreed cynically. His nails cut into his palms as confusion stained her confident gaze. She looked so young and vulnerable he felt a lash of fury. She was nearly thirty—when was she going to toughen up, lose some of her dangerous illusions?

Lowered lashes shielded her eyes. Cabe sighed, despairing inside. He wasn't much good at temporizing. But it was imperative that he mitigate the hurt he'd inflicted on her proud spirit, and in the bargain, get himself away from her sweet eyes without inflicting more.

He dragged in air and expelled it in a raspy laugh. "Okay, so maybe I laid it on a little thick there. Truth is, Sunshine, you're a pretty wench and I like kissing you, too. In fact, I'd like to stand here kissing you from now 'til Monday, but I think I heard Sweet Thing calling me a few minutes ago—"

"Cabe," Laura said warningly, her voice breaking as a wicked grin crinkled his eyes. She found his attempt at playfulness very endearing.

"Laura, I said I wouldn't call him that to his face, didn't I?" Still chuckling, he went upstairs and out the back door.

Laura slumped against the door and shut her eyes. Her whole body throbbed. Lord, how she had wanted him!

It took a moment to strengthen her wobbly legs, and another to recollect what she was here for. Tucking his kiss away to dream on later, she steadied herself with another deep breath. Cabe hadn't said which bedroom needed cleaning out for the nursemaid. Thinking it didn't matter, she chose the one to the right.

There were several opened boxes. Most contained books. Since one end of the paneled room was floor-to-ceiling bookshelves, Laura automatically began filling them.

Having emptied one box, she turned to another, but an open file lying atop a stack of old magazines snagged her glance. It was impossible to resist examining the contents. Newspaper clippings. Cabe and Michele's marriage announcement, an article detailing his decision to turn down a promotion and open his own firm, a card announcing the birth of twins to Mr. and Mrs. Cable J. McClain. Then a sheaf of clippings pertaining to Michele, many with pictures; a vision-in-bridal-white Michele, a chic, suited, chignoned Michele accepting her prestigious position with a noted wildlife conservationist, a tanned, fit, khaki-clad Michele photographing tigers in the wilds of India, snow leopards in the Himalayas, mountain gorillas in Africa, jaguars in Mexico.

Laura paused longest with the one of Michele, glamorous in black velvet and pearls, posing with one of those lavishly illustrated coffee-table books featuring her photographs. Smart, talented, beautiful. Respected. A hard act to follow.

Mentally slapping at her pang of inferiority as if it were a pesky fly, Laura pushed aside the clippings and picked up two colored photographs, an eight-by-ten studio oil of Michele, and a more recent one of Heather. The child's big green eyes were Cabe's, but the golden hair and piquant face were her mother's. Could that be the cause of his somewhat reserved manner with the little girl?

The clippings were in dated order and tracked Michele's career. Why had he kept all this? Was Cabe still torching for his wife? For two years? Of course not. But he was a man who committed himself deeply, Pearl said, which implied a correspondingly deep hurt.

Realizing how seriously she was taking her aunt's astrological analysis of Cabe's character, Laura snorted. Granted, some of it did ring true. But she knew another man who was charmingly warm and kind—as long as it didn't demand anything—and wonderfully generous-hearted, as long as generosity paid dividends. She had been married to him.

"Laura?" Cabe called, causing her to jump. An instant later he appeared in the doorway. "Wrong room," he said.

Her heart pounding, Laura smiled and murmured something about a bad guess. His eyes narrowed. "What's that you're doing?"

"Looking at this file you're keeping up for Heather. I think it's a wonderful idea, Cabe," she replied, casually replacing the clippings.

The seconds ticked by as he stared at her. Then his shoulders relaxed. "I thought when she's older she might be curious, so..." He shrugged. "I'm planning to use this room as an office, not a bedroom."

Several different kinds of relief trembled the knees Laura forced toward the door. "Well, at least you've got a start on all these boxes of books!" she tossed off. "Unfortunately, I can't stick around long enough to do anything to the right bedroom, I've got to get to work. What time do you want me back here?"

I don't even want you to leave, Cabe thought. "Whenever you can make it," he said. He sent her off with a jaunty wave, then shook his head disbelievingly. Hell of a thing, he reflected, when a man hurt less enduring his sweet torment than absenting himself from its source.

Seven

Under the glow of an enormous chandelier, the dining room sparkled with crystal and silver. There was fine china and Irish cream linen. Tall pink tapers rose up from the low arrangements of paler pink roses placed at each end of the long mahogany table, an elegant setting for the four attractive women who comprised half of Cabe's dinner party.

He sat at one end of the table. As hostess, Laura occupied the other end, a satisfying arrangement that gave her an unrestricted view of the handsome host. Feeling exceptionally attractive in her old-new costume—the slim, strapless black sheath was well worn, but the brief white bolero lavished with yards of frilly lace was recently hand-made for her by Dolly—she smiled at Ingrid Hall, the statuesque blond goddess Cabe had placed beside an old friend who was now the editor-in-chief of the local newspaper.

Another satisfying arrangement, Laura thought.

The third woman was the wife of the much older attorney Cabe had chosen to handle his business interests in Fair

Harbor. He and Cord Hunter had decided to co-purchase a large tract of land on Thackary Island, an announcement that was toasted by all, especially Laura.

She had been nervous about meeting Cabe's friends, anxious for them to like and approve of her. To her pleasure, Juliet Dack-Hunter was not at all the intimidating personage she expected. "Susan's told me so much about you, I feel as if I know you, Laura," she said, smiling warmly. "Were you aware that my great-grandfather and your great-grandmother were close friends?"

Relaxing, Laura replied, "Yes, I know. In fact, I inherited the lovely little tulipwood writing desk he made for her. It still has the original satin-pewter pulls."

Intrigued, Juliet asked if she could see it. "First thing tomorrow," Laura replied. She felt vitally alive and was delighted when Cabe suggested they wind up the evening dancing. The Three Oaks' Gold Room featured live music until eleven, which gave them forty minutes if they hurried.

In the end only she and Cabe and the Hunters wound up at the Gold Room. The handsome couple headed for the dance floor immediately after they had ordered drinks. Standing up, Cabe stretched out a hand to Laura.

"Shall we?"

"Can you?"

Lazily arrogant, he tipped back his head and smiled. "I can do anything I put my mind to," he informed her. "Besides, it's slow-dancing," he continued, leading her to the floor. "If done correctly, you can dance all night without ever moving anything below the knees. And naturally I do it right."

He's certainly feeling good, Laura thought. Playing up to his mood, she let him capture her fingertips and whirl her into his embrace. Then, her smile sultry, she slipped one hand into his and held it between them. The other she placed primly on his shoulder.

The lighting was dim, the atmosphere romantic. The song they swayed to was "That Old Black Magic." Laura thought it marvelously appropriate. Scant inches separated the fluid softness of her thighs from the hardness of his. That tiny bit of space seemed to glow with a radiance that acted like a stimulant on her nerves. The magnetic attraction Cabe exerted pulled at her senses, drawing her ever closer. Potently aware of her femininity, she wanted to flirt, to arouse and seduce. Reclaiming her hand, she slid her fingertips along his wide shoulders. They met in the crisp, dark curls at his nape.

Languidly, she stroked through the springy thatch, and trailed three fingers caressingly down to his collar then back up again. She curved her arm around his neck and fitted her body smoothly to his.

The song ended, and the band swung smoothly into another one. Eyes closed, Laura raised her face until Cabe's clean-shaven cheek lay against hers. The temptation to trace his strong-boned contours with her lips was nearly irresistible. She nestled closer and felt his mouth trail across her temple before coming to rest in her hair.

She had swept the softly curling mass to one side. Cabe inhaled slowly as his mouth came into contact with her skin. The excitement that stirred him was mixed with a kind of incredulous joy. Her supple body followed every cant and sway of his. His steps, though uneven, felt light instead of clumsy. In some mysterious way she had given him back his sense of grace.

Nevertheless, dancing with Laura, he discovered, was just another way to torment himself. Every masculine cell of him was aware of the woman he held in his arms. He could feel the shape of her breasts through his thin silk shirt. Her hips moved to his rhythm tantalizingly. His imagination roamed as wildly as his hands ached to do. He kept them firmly on her waist, but in his mind they slid down and gripped the mounded curves of her bottom. He closed his eyes and mentally crushed her against him while he took her red mouth in a wild rage of hunger....

Realizing that his hands were actually moving, he inwardly shuddered and locked them loosely on her back. Cabe, he chastised himself, you're not thinking like her friend and protector. You're thinking like a man.

The music stopped. They had a drink, changed partners, then danced the final set together. Laura's eyes were luminous dark stars as they left the Oaks. Cabe figured he'd do just about anything to keep that look on her face. Throwing aside restraint and a large measure of dignity, he began pleading an unbearable craving for a hot, crusty, mushroom-pepperoni-double-cheese-double-crust pizza that was not only ridiculous, but insanely contagious. Locating an open pizza place was cause for wild jubilation.

Laura was already riding a tremendous high. Her spirits rose stratospherically as they sat at an oilcloth-covered table greedily consuming pitchers of icy beer and great, caloric rounds of ambrosia while Juliet's roguish husband regaled them with feats of derring-do. Most of these seemed to consist mainly of slinging his woman over his shoulder and carrying her off to his castle with her kicking and screaming all the way... well, for five minutes, anyhow.

Juliet's response was a gorgeously haughty sniff. Laura thought she could warm her hands in the glow the other couple gave off. Cabe, though obviously enjoying his friend's nonsensical claims, appeared serenely immune to the emotions storming her heart. Feeling transparently vulnerable, she concentrated on cleaning her cheese-smeared fingers.

Outside again, Juliet assessed the two high-spirited males and sensibly decided she would drive. They all went a bit crazy on the ride home and the car rang with absurdities and laughter. By the time they reached River Street, Laura was literally aching from happiness.

A different kind of ache pulsed its demands as she was flung against Cabe during a sharp curve. He held her until she had righted herself. She wanted to keep his arms around her. She wanted desperately to be kissed and consoled her needful self by anticipating a few moments alone with him at her door.

"We'll drop Laura off first. She's running a marathon tomorrow morning and has to be up at the crack of dawn," Cabe said, chuckling.

"Oh, Cabe, it's just a 10-K race and, anyway, I decided against it." Laura laughed, blinking furiously. "It's all I can do to find the kitchen at the crack of dawn, much less a race on the other side of Wilmington! But I am getting sleepy," she said with a delicate yawn.

Fatigue enveloped her as she walked into the cottage and the yawn became real. Wearily she knelt to cuddle KK. Wild with joy, the tiny animal followed her into the bedroom, and with only a little coaxing, into bed.

Laura needed something to hold. Her lovely excitement had evaporated by the time she turned out her bedroom lights. Her eyes still smarted with the grit of disappointment. Serves you right, she berated herself, letting yourself get carried away like that. She slid deeper into the covers. Had she acted the seductive fool on the dance floor? Probably so. She tried to recollect her actual behavior, but a velvety black fog swept down to obliterate the power of reason.

KK was up at first light and out his pet door. It was after eleven when his mistress emerged into brilliant sunshine. Last night's disappointment had bounced off her resilient young heart. Attired in a red crop-top and knee-length knickers, her hair caught up high and tied with a folded print scarf, she looked as vibrant as she felt.

Shading her eyes, she called for KK, but the dog was nowhere to be seen. Probably kidnapped by Heather, she thought. Laughing to herself, Laura ran lightly across the connecting lawns, her quickness betraying an eagerness that had little to do with rescuing her pet.

She took the path that led around to the back of the house. Passing under the ferny branches of a young mimosa, she stopped with a soft, indrawn breath.

Delight drenched her. Barefoot and shirtless, his back against the wall and knee upraised, Cabe sat on the terrace holding a baby.

One bent arm and outspread hand supported the infant's wriggly body. The other hand cradled its fragile head. With beguiling delicacy, the big man touched his cheek to the baby's.

Tears stung Laura's eyelids. The powerful man, the tiny boy-child, the infinitely gentle caress. She felt profoundly stirred by the tender tableau. She had wondered how hard Cabe had taken the loss of his son. Now, intuitively, she knew, and compassion gripped her heart.

Just then Juliet came out and claimed her baby. Laughing, Cabe released him and stood up. "He's a great little kid," he said huskily. "Won't be anytime before ole Cord'll be out buying baseball bats and fishing poles!"

"Ole Cord's *already* been out buying baseball bats and fishing poles. He even brought a baseball glove to the hospital," she said, and they laughed together.

Cabe held the door open for her. Then, still unaware of his audience, he walked to the edge of the terrace and raised his hands high above his head in a sinuous stretch.

Laura went as still as the garden sculpture that centered a nearby lily pond. A shivery sensation, hot and cold at once, raced down her body. He stood with legs wide apart, his back arched, his skin pulled taut over firm, corded flesh. As he stretched to his full height, the sensuous play of muscles rippling across his wide shoulders and down his back held her entranced.

Totally unself-conscious, he linked his fingers and leisurely turned, presenting her with a view that liquified her bones. Except for the soft nest of curls at the base of his throat, his chest was as smooth as a sheet of copper.

Her breath came quick as she imagined kissing a trail from his flat brown nipples to his drum-hard stomach. The sleek line of hair that began just below his navel grew thicker and more luxuriant as it arrowed downward and slid beneath his low-slung jeans. Knowing he'd spot her any second, she tried to calm her throbbing pulses, but desire and pride were a heady mix. He was tall and golden and magnificently male.

Shaking free of her trance, she pushed aside the mimosa fronds just as narrowing green eyes registered her presence.

Cabe straightened and shot his hands into his hip pockets, thumbs out. "What are you lookin' at, Sunshine?" he asked with an amused tilt of lips.

That lazy arrogance was back. Laura swallowed.

"Something wonderful."

His amusement hardened.

"You mean that bit with the baby?"

"Yes, that, too. You're a beautiful man, Cabe," she said softly. "Beautiful inside and out."

Cabe snorted. Laura quickly looked away, but he caught the wink of dimples. Crossing to the wrought-iron table that held a cornucopia of fresh fruit, he chose a piece and wiped it on his thigh.

Laura walked up the steps, drawn to his side. "Is KK about?"

"Inside." Letting his gaze play over the ripe curves of her, he sank his teeth through the winey skin and juicy white flesh of a crisp mountain apple.

She cupped her hands. "Toss me one?"

Complying, he lowered his frame into a chair and propped his feet up on the low stone wall that encircled the terrace. Laura sat down beside him. "How do you feel?" she inquired.

"Like I had a tad too much to drink last night."

"Ummm." She bit into the tart fruit.

He cut her a sideways glance. "So did you, I think."

"No. I had only the one glass of dinner wine. Anything I did last night was done with faculties intact."

Cabe took another huge bite of apple.

With a whoop of delight, Heather burst out the door behind them, KK at her heels. He leaped into Laura's lap and pranced around before settling in.

Heather clambered onto her father's knees. "Miss Richards, guess what!"

His mouth twitching, Cabe scowled at his daughter. "Give us a break, huh? No more 'guess whats' for at least five minutes. Here, have an apple."

"I don't want an apple."

"Have one anyway. Here." Cabe lifted her onto his lap and pointed at the river spreading as far as the eye could see. "See those green humps way over there?"

"You mean those tiny baby islands?"

"Those are isles." Cabe's voice lowered nearly to a whisper. "Pirate isles. Blackbeard used to roam all around here, they say, hiding out after he'd sacked and looted and sank the swift, white-masted sailing ships that plied the Atlantic. Made them all walk the plank, old Blackbeard did. Then he'd come here to bury his treasures. Old-timers say there're treasure chests hidden all over this area, in those isles, along the beaches. And sometimes, if you look real quick, you just might see the ghost of that fierce pirate walking the beach, shaking his fist at all these people come to hunt his treasure."

"Oh, Daddy," Heather said, giggling. But she couldn't remain the skeptic for long. "Can *we* go hunting for treasure?"

"You bet. Next weekend, maybe." He glanced at Laura. "You think Miss Richards might want to come help us hunt?"

"You bet!" Laura said. Laughing, feeling adrift in that dangerous minefield of happiness again, she reached over to link fingers with Heather.

Cabe tensed. Her arm crossed his, and the womanly muscles cupped in soft, rounded flesh lay sweet on his naked skin. The air was hot and swept with perfume-laden breezes. On his tongue the tangy taste of apple mingled with the smell of sea salt and the dark, exciting scent of fertile earth, and, lacing through it like a sensuous ribbon, the flower-garden sultriness of Laura.

He glanced at her lips, and his mouth remembered the pleasure to be found there. Irresistibly, his gaze fell lower. Her innocent forward lean revealed a curving scrap of black lace and the beginning swell of her breasts. Desire flamed up in him.

"Now, Daddy?" Heather asked hopefully, interrupting her father's thoughts.

"Now."

"Miss Richards—"

"No guess whats. Just tell her."

The little girl's pout reversed to an excited smile as she wheeled to Laura. "Daddy's coming back to Raleigh with us, is what. Because I'm in a play Tuesday night and he wouldn't miss it for anything! Then he's going to New York for business and then he's coming back Thursday night—" she gulped air "—and then we're coming home. Friday we don't have classes," she explained.

Shyly she twisted her hair ribbon. "In the play I'm a little green frog. You want to come see me hop and go ribbet! ribbet!?"

"That sounds like such fun. But I've got so much work to do this week," Laura said with genuine regret. "This coming weekend is Country Craft Days at our store."

"What's that?" Cabe asked, intrigued.

"It's a tradition started by my grandmother. Pearl's taken it over now, bigger and better than ever, she says. It starts Friday morning and runs till Sunday evening," Laura said.

About that time KK leaped from her lap and streaked across the yard. "That squirrel," Heather said knowingly, taking off after the dog.

Cabe strolled to the edge of the terrace and jammed his hands into his hip pockets again, saying abruptly, "I've asked John Ed to keep an eye on things while I'm gone."

"What time are you leaving?" Laura asked, her voice steady even though she felt a sinking sensation in her stomach.

"Around one. We're making a raid on the refrigerator first. You're welcome to join us if you'd like. In fact, why don't you invite Dolly and Pearl?" he suggested carelessly. "There's enough leftover food in there to feed a regiment."

"Thank you, Cabe, they'd love that." Coming to his side, Laura laid her palm feather-light on his sun-warmed shoulder. She felt so close to him just then. "But why don't you call them? It'd mean more, coming from you."

He walked out from under her hand. "Look, if you want them, then call them. Don't make a big deal out of this."

Her chin whipped up. "If that's the way you feel, maybe we'd just better forget the whole idea, including myself."

"Oh, come on now," Cabe said, his irritation shading into concern. He tugged at her hair. "You go in and call them. Go on, call them and tell them . . . tell them we need some of Dolly's fantastic bread if she's got any. Go, go," he said, making little shooing motions. He cocked his head, assessing KK's altered barking. Green eyes twinkled. "I've got a dog to get down from a tree!"

He swung down the steps, a bravado gesture. Noting the proud set of his dark head and conversely, his hampered stride, Laura kept her mouth clamped shut. She wanted to call after him, with some sassy rejoinder to let him know what she thought of his quicksilver mood changes. But her emotions were too unsettled to trust herself to speak. Pivoting, she went inside to call Dolly and Pearl.

As expected, their pleasure was unbounded at being included in the lively party that developed around the impromptu luncheon. Much later that day, sitting on the cottage terrace enjoying a spectacular sunset, Dolly said musingly, "I thought the rich were supposed to be stuck-up snobs. Cabe's climbed pretty high up the ladder himself. But everyone was so nice and friendly... What's that Ingrid person like?"

"The kind of woman who makes you aware that you've got a pin in your bra strap and she's got x-ray vision," Laura responded dryly.

Pearl looked appalled. "You had a pin in your bra strap?"

"No, of course not, that's just an expression." Still chuckling, Laura let her attention drift gently away to the house next door. She could feel its emptiness as an inner chill. *I miss him already.* "I'm sorry, what were you saying, Aunt Pearl?"

"I was saying what fun I've had this week getting ready for Country Craft Days. Judging from what I've seen so far, I'm willing to predict we're going to make a bundle this year!" Hazel eyes shining, Pearl added proudly, "And I know what we'll do with the profits, too. Since Laura already has the money for my surgery, this'll go toward paying off the yogurt machine."

Laura smiled to herself. She doubted a craft show would improve their fortunes all that much. "Lord knows I wish you success," she said. "Mmm, what a gorgeous evening! If you wouldn't mind giving me a ride to the dock, Aunt Pearl, I'd like to pick up my boat, see how it runs since John Ed's tinkered with it. Maybe I'll even ride off into the sunset," she jested, her laugh unconsciously wistful as she gazed at the luminous green islets floating on a molten sea. They reminded her of Cabe's eyes when he was looking at her and thought she didn't know it.

Eight

Friday morning Cabe woke with a sense of boundless energy. Striding to the kitchen to make coffee, he thought about taking a bike ride, ten, maybe fifteen miles. Hell, maybe even twenty! No. Cancel the bike ride. He couldn't leave Heather alone in the house. She might wake up and be frightened. A potential future problem there, he conceded. But he felt too good to worry about future problems.

He sang in the shower and whistled while he shaved. Dressing in chino slacks, he paused at the mirror to run a comb through his damp hair. Anticipation. That's what fueled his vibrant good feelings. That, and an easing somewhere at the back of his mind. What had changed? He shrugged. His mood wasn't geared to analysis. Taking the stairs two at a time, he went outside to collect the newspaper.

The air tasted like fruity wine and he drank in great draughts of it. He was glad to be alive, glad that his bare feet were drenched with dew, that he had bought this house and all these trees and the lamppost's vining white jasmine with its extravagant perfume! He'd forgotten how it felt to feel so damned *good*.

"Daddy?" a sleepy voice floated down the stairs and out the open door.

"Coming, baby...ouch, damn it!" he muttered, hopping about as he tried to massage the foot that had come into bristly contact with a pine cone. A low, throaty ripple of laughter reached his ears. He wheeled, his heart turning cartwheels as he tracked the enchanting sound to a flash of dimples and laughing dark eyes. Dressed in a full-skirted frock of calico and lace, Laura stood under a tree that rained white flowers with every passing breeze. He was entranced.

She moistened her lips. "Hi, Cabe."

Cabe stared at her wonderingly. How could such simple little words ricochet through him like that? "Hi, yourself," he said, his voice painfully husky. She looked so pretty in her tight-waisted dress. With that mass of curls wreathing her vivid face, the flower-sprigged, wine and cream calico lent her the timeless appeal of a vibrant young maid.

Her rosy mouth curved as their gazes met and locked. He gravitated toward her with a naturalness that set off an inner alarm. It registered, but dimly. Her head arched back as he approached, revealing the clean lines of her throat and the throbbing little hollow he ached to kiss and go on kissing until he reached her breasts....

Irritably, Cabe curbed his runaway thoughts. Why did he keep forgetting that he had no right to feel this way?

But her huge eyes fired him with the longing to take her in his arms and hold her warm and close. Tiny white blossoms starred her dusky hair. Ever so gently he brushed them away, then grinned and tweaked a bouncy curl. "How you doing, Sunshine? As good as you look, I hope!"

"I'm doing fine, thank you," Laura replied a little testily. She had just realized the reason for his occasional use of her nickname. It relegated her to the safe status of a little girl.

Lazily she lowered her lashes to the slim hand taking possession of her arm. "You're looking pretty good, too," she said, smiling at her understatement.

Her fingertips air-brushed from his wrist to his elbow and back. A wry smile tucked into his lips as Cabe followed their warm progress. She touched, patted, stroked and hugged so naturally, innocently. His desire to reciprocate was so erotic he felt he should be ashamed of himself, making his struggle to keep his hands off her one of almost comical desperation. Casually he slid the itchy hands into his hip pockets.

Laughing a little, Laura looked up at him. "I trust you missed me while you were gone?"

"Like five rainy days in a row," he teased.

"Dad–dy!" a petulant voice rang out. "I want some breakfuss!"

The two adults shared an amused look. "I think that's a direct order," Cabe murmured.

"I think so, too. One you'd best obey," Laura replied, chuckling. "Are you coming down to the store today?"

"Wouldn't miss it," he declared.

With a pleased laugh and a swirl of ruffled skirts, she left him. Her hair swung in mesmerizing cadence to swaying hips. The peak-a-boo play of petticoats dancing around her slender legs caught at the masculine heart. Only after she disappeared through the hedge did Cabe bow to the tyranny of his daughter's command.

Heather was coming out the door when he reached it. Without a word he picked her up, tucked her upside down under one arm and carried her squealing and giggling up the stairs to dump her unceremoniously on her bed.

"There's no food in the house so we'll have to eat downtown," he said. That suited her. His choice of attire didn't. Placing her hands on miniature hips, she vetoed the frilly pink dress he selected in favor of yellow overalls and matching knit shirt.

Since he yielded the victory early in the battle, the matter was settled without too much strain on their relationship. Then he took a brush to her tangled tresses and warfare erupted again, far more noisily this time. Cabe was a fatherly wreck by the time he finished restoring his daughter's hair to order.

Though none too dexterous with ribbons, he managed to fashion a bow, which she said was too floppy and people would laugh. Declaring it a perfectly respectable bow, he started looking for her red sneakers. They were under the bed. When he went down on his knees to reach them, she jumped on his back and locked her arms lovingly around his neck before sprawling beside him to put on the recovered shoes.

Cabe sat back on his haunches and gazed at her thoughtfully. Maybe Laura was right, he conceded, wincing as he imagined going through this routine every morning. Maybe he did need live-in help.

"Let me put some shoes on and we'll be off," he said, getting to his feet. He slipped on moccasins and pulled out a favorite shirt he hadn't worn since his accident, a South Seas print featuring red and yellow parrots on a blue background.

Heather thought it was yukky. Laura did, too. "Cabe, that shirt," she sighed when they walked into the crowded store.

Deciding to take that as a compliment, Cabe flicked off an imaginary piece of lint. "Pretty neat, huh? I bought it in Brazil." He grinned at Dolly, who, evading his gaze, hurriedly scooped up Heather and bore her off. Crinkling green eyes cut back at Laura. "Looks like a pretty good turnout. I'm in the market for something or other—want to give me the guided tour?"

"I'd love to, but Cabe, you know you're not required to buy anything." Her nose wrinkled beguilingly. "However, if by chance you do happen to find something you simply can't live without, I'll be delighted to ring it up for you! Ready?''

Her saucy smile knotted his stomach. "Ready," he said, though what he really wanted to do was snatch her up and run off, a startling caveman urge that tickled his fancy in spite of its absurdity.

Warm greetings accompanied their progress through the room. Speculative looks abounded, which he found more amusing than offensive.

"Laura, this is really something!" he said, genuinely impressed as they stopped just inside the open glass doors of the transformed storage room. John Ed had laid planks across unopened cartons and draped the resulting shelves with heavy blue fabric. One side was given to a fascinating array of handicrafts that ranged from the silly to the sublime. But it was the food display that captured Cabe's attention.

Jars of ruby and topaz jams and jellies shimmered on the peacock-blue cloth. Assorted pickles, red, yellow and a dozen shades of green, backlit their jewellike hues. Small crocks of home-churned butter captured the sunlight. Crusty brown loaves in every shape and size from long to oval to an enormous pumpernickel round spilled artfully from baskets, studded suggestively with pear, plum and peach preserves.

There were sheets of frosted brownies, and six different kinds of cookies, double-chocolate cakes with fudge icing piled on in thick swirls, vanilla creme, spicy carrot, and old-fashioned pineapple upside-down cakes. To enhance the festival air, there was cotton candy. Heather was already nose-deep in the airy pink stuff.

Cabe felt like a kid in a candy store with a pocketful of pennies. He bought pickles and sausage and breads and jams; cookies, three varieties, and a chocolate cake. He bought a Raggedy Ann doll restored by a woman's patient hand, good as new. "And these two deer," he said, running a caressing hand over a ten-inch tall stag and doe carved from golden pine.

A black, white and orange live kitten from the basket placed strategically near the door was added to the list. Cabe didn't have much choice in the matter; his daughter fell head over heels in love with the tiny charmer. "A house isn't a home without a cat lying in front of the fireplace," he defended his indulgence.

"We're going treasure hunting today. It's the only way I'll be able to drag Heather out of here," he admitted ruefully, evoking a husky laugh from Laura. It pleased her immensely that he seemed so much more at ease with his parental role. "Want to come with us?"

"Wish I could," Laura declined lightly, a difficult task when inside she was jumping up and down and yelling yes, yes, yes! She watched him with a soft and painful delight. His usually somber face was alive with pleasure. Why he had returned in this effervescent mood was another mystery, but the eyes sparkling between their lashes were free of the bitter cynicism that shadowed them at times, and she'd give a lot to keep them like that.

"Miss Richards, did you see my kitty?" Heather crowed. "I'm going to name her Melissa!"

"A beautiful name for her," Laura declared.

"Him. It's a boy cat. At least I hope so," Cabe muttered. He tilted his head. "Sure you can't steal away and come with us? It'll probably be two or so before we leave for the beach."

"Of course she can," Dolly answered for her. "We've got enough volunteers here to run a county fair! So you just go on, honey, have yourself some fun."

"Well, if you're sure, Aunt Dolly," Laura murmured, abashed at how easily she was persuaded. "We could take my boat if you'd like, Cabe. It's a gorgeous run out to Long Beach—"

"Please, Daddy, let's go in the car?" Heather requested.

"Maybe another time for the boat," Laura said quickly. "I'll meet you out at the house about two, then?"

"Two it is," Cabe said. "Come along, Heather. No, kitties do not like beaches," Laura heard him say emphatically as they walked out the door.

At two o'clock she was in her bedroom changing into last year's swim suit and a pink cotton cover-up styled like a man's shirt. Sliding her feet into beach thongs, she grabbed up KK and rushed outside in response to Cabe's car horn.

"KK's going?"

"Yes, he is," Laura said. "He loves the beach."

"Oh, good!" came a cry from the back seat. Being a sensible man, Cabe shut up.

His attire was casual—a sleeveless, paint-stained sweatshirt and cutoffs. Laura glanced at him every chance she got. Listening to Heather's piping chatter interspersed with his husky laughter, she felt a dangerous expansion of heart. Settle down, girl, she warned herself. But just seeing him again had suffused her with joyous excitement. Contemplating an entire afternoon with this laughing, teasing, utterly irresistible male created a wild singing in her blood.

Resolutely she focused her gaze out the window, which was not that much of a hardship; for the narrow beach road ran through some spectacular scenery. To her left, towering sand dunes blocked the pounding Atlantic. On the right, beige sand beaches flowed into serene, sailboat-dotted lagoons.

Regardless of how often she saw it, Laura was always stirred by the area's wildly contrarious beauty. She was out of the car as soon as they stopped, splashing down the ribbon of sand and froth with Heather and the dog racing the wind beside her. Wheeling, they ran back to meet Cabe. Heather and KK detoured to the ankle-deep water, but she went on.

Spinning a circle around him, she threw out her hands delightedly. "Oh, Cabe! Isn't it *lovely*!"

"Lovely," Cabe said, his voice unsteady. As she gazed up at him, he saw the strange mixture that had beguiled and confused him so before, the child Laura peeking out through a desirable woman's eyes.

"Well, come on, slowpoke, let's go!" she cajoled. Whirling again, she danced off a few steps, then stopped and flung a hand to her mouth with a stricken look. "Oh, Cabe, I forgot—I'm sorry!"

Cabe swore softly. But this time his inner rage was for her distress, not his handicap. Casting about for something to ease the awkward moment, he agreed indignantly, "Well, I guess so! Here I am, a handicapped person braving the sea-and-sand fury of a wilderness beach," he charged, glaring around the placid lagoon filled with children and toy boats and a dog or two, "burdened down like a pack mule—and what do I get for my efforts? Gratitude? Compassion? A tiny bit of well-deserved pity? No, I get yelled at and called *slowpoke*," he wound up so aggrievedly she burst out laughing.

"All right, I apologize! Here." She took half of his burdens, a colorful sand pail and shovel. Her vivid face sobered. "Cabe, I am sorry."

"So am I. I'd like to run like that again, chase a pretty girl down the beach again," Cabe said, grinning as his gaze flowed down her legs. "But I can't. Maybe I never will." He shrugged, fatalistic.

"Oh, Cabe, I wish—" she began, gazing at him with too shiny eyes.

His flinted. "Wishes don't count, Sunshine. Now lighten up. Besides, maybe I ought to be the one commiserating with you, the way you bounce along..." Making a tsk-tsk sound through his teeth, Cabe tossed down the towels and stripped off his shirt while she sputtered deliciously.

His lashes screened his eyes as he watched her scoop up the sand pail and fleetly deliver it to Heather. Never in all the months since his accident had he felt the ungainliness of his stride so acutely.

Wadding his shirt into a ball, he threw it atop the towels. "I think I'll swim off the Point for a while," he said.

"I'll stay here and keep an eye on things." Laura unbuttoned her shirt as she spoke. When she peeled it off, Cabe felt a weakness in his midsection. She wore a one-piece black suit styled with a pleated white organdy ruffle running from one shoulder to the modest vee between her breasts. A bikini couldn't hold a candle to the sex appeal she exuded, he thought. Wheeling, he stripped off his shorts and sneakers.

Laura's breath caught in her throat as she admired his smooth-muscled back and long-limbed torso. When he turned, she felt an electric shock at the arrogance with which he filled his slick white trunks. He was beautiful.

Her wordless sound jerked his head around. Her liquid gaze collided with the hot green flint of his eyes and held for a throbbing moment. Unable to bear the tension any longer, she shattered it with a sibilant breath. Turning sharply, he strode toward the jutting spit of land.

Preferring to observe rather than participate, Laura spread a towel and stretched out on her stomach. The warm, shallow seabed deepened rapidly at the Point and soon all she could see of Cabe was a sleek dark head and powerful arms slicing through the water.

Then he returned and stole up behind Heather with a dragon's roar. She squealed delightedly and the chase was on. Gradually he took her out deeper until the water reached her tiny waist. Laura dug her chin into folded arms and dreamily watched.

Cabe lifted his giggling daughter high in the air and let her come swooshing down, taking care to keep her head above water. Then he tripped and accidently ducked her. Heather popped to the top of the water with a strangled wail. He grabbed and held her while she sputtered and wiped her face. "Dad-dy! Why did you do that to me? That was *mean*," she cried.

Sliding an arm under her small bottom, Cabe raised her to shoulder level. Her mouth quivered. His voice was rough velvet. "Baby, I didn't do that to you on purpose. It was an accident—you know I'm not mean."

Heather obstinately shut her eyes and ears. "I want down. Put me down, please."

Cabe carefully set her down.

Laura had come to her feet at the first wail. Reacting to the man's distress as well as the child's, she plunged into the water and laughingly intercepted Heather's dash for land. Thankful for the small hand curling into hers, she leaned down to the little girl's level.

"Of course your daddy wasn't being mean, and sure, it was an accident. But he's in a lot of trouble just the same! Do you know why?" Eyes wary, Heather shook her head. Laura lowered her voice to a conspiratory whisper. "Because sometimes accidents can turn into a lot of fun. Want to see what I mean?"

This time Heather nodded. Grinning, Laura met Cabe's watchful eyes. Before he could react, she reached out and pushed his head under water. He came up sputtering and roaring. "The best part of this game is that we can duck him, but he can't do a thing to us!" she told Heather gleefully. "It's the rule—boys can't duck girls, ha!"

An instant later he was under water again. Heather began to giggle. Laura joined in as he shot out of the water with outlandish threats of revenge he couldn't make good on. "Who made that rule, anyway?" he wanted to know.

"I did," Laura said. "I made that rule."

"And me," said Heather. Tentatively at first, then with gleeful aggressiveness, she surged up to where Cabe sat neck deep in water, and pushed his head under. His growls ferocious, he thrashed around in the water like some great beast they had to capture, resulting in much running and dashing about.

When the two adults tired of the extensive waterplay, KK took over, leading Heather a merry chase for possession of a stick he'd found. Laura and Cabe stretched out on towels, he on his back, propped up on his elbows, she in her former position, facing him.

"You were okay out there once you got the hang of it," she mused, curving her legs up over her bottom to wave in the air. "But you were so awkward at first—haven't you played water games with her before?"

Cabe's mouth went awry. "I've been a little busy lately, remember? Lord, Heather!" he protested as she plopped her gritty self atop his midriff.

"That was fun, Daddy!" she declared. "And I'm not mad at you anymore, either."

"Ah. Miss Richards the wizard to the rescue again," Cabe intoned. He pulled Heather down until, with a tired sigh, she rested her head on his chest. KK came romping up and curled up in the crook of Laura's arm.

"Déjù vu," he said, stroking his daughter's hair. "Did you know I used to bring Laura and whatever dog she had at the time here to play when she was a little girl? She was only a few years older than you at the time. Which is all the more reason..." His gaze captured alert dark eyes and held fast.

Laura didn't need him to finish the sentence. She could finish it herself. Her soft mouth firmed. He was still using their youthful relationship as a barbed-wire fence between them. Lightly, she rebutted, "Your daddy forgot to mention that he was little more than a boy himself at the time. Strong and responsible, to be sure, but still a boy. Although what that had to do with anything I don't know. Eventually he grew up and so did she—"

"Did she?" Cabe cut in. He smiled as he assessed the point of his question. She sat Indian-fashion, holding her dog, strands of wet hair whipping around her sun-flushed cheeks.

Her eyes flashed. "Yes, she did."

He laughed, aching to draw her down beside Heather and hold her. "Physically, yes. But in many ways she's still very much the innocent when compared with that boy. Love, marriage, parenthood, divorce; he's had all that and is sensibly persuaded that once is enough. But not her. Despite her own sour experience with love, she's still waiting for her prince to come. Am I right, Sunshine?''

His tone was lightly sarcastic. His eyes were disturbingly intense. Laura struggled to insert reason into her dizzying mix of emotions. She felt elated; this was the first time he had spoken freely of his personal convictions. But their negative slant canceled out pleasure. Confusedly she wondered what he wanted from her, what kind of an answer he was hoping to get. And why was it so important to him, as his unblinking gaze implied?

On the heels of her thought, he relaxed and merely looked amused. Pride forced her careless response. "Oh, come on, Cabe, you're not that much of a cynic," she sniffed. Was he? She prayed not. "I'm not that much of a believer in princes, either. If it happens, then it happens. If it doesn't . . ." She lifted what she hoped to be a convincingly eloquent shoulder.

"Hmm." Cabe dribbled a handful of hot sand down her arm. "What about all that pattering of little feet you were trying to sell me on that first day?"

Laura hesitated fractionally. Was there a false note in that teasing voice? Confused by her own intuitive senses, she retorted, "Well, you're the one with the big house and the money to afford all those expensive little feet."

Something streaked his eyes and was gone. He laughed, a real laugh, and turned his attention to Heather. Becoming bored with adult conversation that didn't make much sense anyway, the little girl had wandered off to find her shovel. The missing object in hand, she squatted beside him and started digging for buried treasure.

Cabe joined her. Laura stayed where she was. Her reaction to his last few remarks still puzzled her. Why did she instinctively shrink from exposing to him her intense desire for children? Not exposure, she corrected. Sharing. Why do I feel so wary about sharing the maternal part of myself with him? "Oh, give me that other shovel," she sighed, finding no answer to her question.

Apparently Blackbeard had bypassed the spot. "Next time we'll dig over there by the big rock," Cabe said briskly. "Time to pack it in now. It's getting late and I'm hungry."

Heather was hungry, too, but she wanted to climb a sand mountain before they left. Agreeably, Cabe scooped her up and started toward the dunes.

"Cabe, wait a minute, maybe we ought to leave that for another time. It can get pretty rough trying to keep your footing on these crumbly things." Laura immediately wished she hadn't said it. Her remark struck Cabe as a challenge rather than concerned advice. You should have known better, she scolded herself as he crossed the road with Heather astride his shoulders. That prickly male ego!

They all had to struggle to scale the perpendicular dune. Linking fingers, they paused on top for a panoramic view that held Heather's interest for all of ten seconds. Thunderous waves and wind prevented conversation. Giving up, they followed the grubby little figure back down the sand hill's wind-sculpted flank.

As predicted, it crumbled underfoot, sending them lurching this way and that. Heather's downward progress involved falling and rolling and peals of gleeful laughter. Cabe's whooping descent wasn't much better, and Laura, feeling young and carefree, ended up in a breathless heap that had her performing a mid-air leap to avoid landing on top of the child.

"That was insane, Cabe!" she charged.

Brushing wildly at the sand coating her hair and face, she turned to look at him and lunged to her feet with a choked gasp. Cabe was still sitting there, his laughter frozen into an agonized grimace.

Nine

_____

Laura's heart thudded, thick, slow beats that seemed to freeze her muscles as she struggled to her feet. "Cabe! What's wrong?" she cried.

"I think I've sprained my ankle," he said though clenched teeth.

She dropped to her knees beside him. "How bad is it? Does it hurt? What a stupid question—of course it hurts!" she berated herself. His features were drawn with pain. "Oh, Cabe, it's your bad leg, too! Where all does it hurt—just your ankle, or is it your whole leg? Do you think you've injured it, too?"

"I don't think so, but I'm not going to find out sitting here," he rasped.

"I'll run and get the car. You sit right here, don't try to get up," she instructed briskly. Her legs had turned to mush. How in the world was she going to get them as far as the car? "Where are the keys?"

"In my jacket pocket."

Stumbling away from him, she muttered agitatedly, "What jacket?"

After what seemed a small eternity, she had everyone in the car and was on the road again. "Laura, for God's sake, slow down before we all need a doctor! It's not as if I'm dying," Cabe said as she took a corner on two wheels.

His valiant jest shook her voice. "But you're hurting. I can't stand it when someone's hurting. There's an emergency clinic at the end of Maxwell Street—be there in a jiffy. In one piece, too."

Ignoring his grunt, she focused her attention on Heather, who sat big-eyed and subdued in the back seat. Laura thought it a good idea to have the child stay with Dolly while they were at the clinic. Cabe didn't argue.

Laura wheeled into the loading zone in front of the store, motor running. "Just tell Aunt Dolly you're to stay here until I come back for you, honey," she instructed. "I'll explain everything then."

"I'm glad you thought of that," Cabe said as they left the clinic nearly an hour later. "It was bad enough that you had to sit there all that time."

"I didn't mind." Pain still tautened his features. Apparently his medication hadn't taken effect yet. "I'm just glad the damages were limited to a sprained ankle," she rushed on. "Not that a sprained ankle's anything to sneeze at and I know your whole leg's throbbing from that wrenching fall—"

"Laura, I know what you mean, and I thank you for your concern," he cut in with a thin smile, "but let's get on to something else. I've got to make some plans here."

"I know, I've been thinking about that and I've got it all figured out."

"Why doesn't that surprise me?" Cabe said, but despite his sardonic tone, he felt strangely lighthearted at being the object of her concern. "So tell me what you've come up with."

After telling him, she had to go through it again with Dolly. "Cabe's waiting in the car so let's be quick about this. He has strict orders to keep off his feet as much as possible, which means someone needs to stay at the house, to see to Heather if nothing else. Aunt Pearl and I have to be at the store keeping track of sales, but I can take the night shift with Cabe and you take the day."

Troubled, Pearl said, "Laura, honey, I'm not sure it's fitting that you stay there alone with him at night."

"Oh, Pearl, of course it's fitting, this is the eighties," Dolly reproved, then exchanged an astonished look with her sister-in-law at this reversal of attitudes. "Besides, evenings are the best times for a woman to show off her domestic and maternal skills. Here, honey," she said to Laura, "there's the fixings of a good supper in this sack, but you don't have to tell him that. Just let him think you fixed it."

"Aunt Dolly, do you ever stop?" Laura sighed as she took the sack. Thanking both aunts with a loving kiss on the cheek, she escorted Heather and KK back to the car.

Dusk was hanging purple shadows around the big house when they arrived. Though Laura itched to assist Cabe, she went upstairs and left him to make it alone. She whisked their soiled towels into the clothes hamper, then casually entered the den at the same time he did.

Cabe stopped and stared at her, the vivid face, the wind-tossed romp of silky hair, her lovely legs and small bare feet. Unaware of how desirable she looked to the man who depended on the support of crutches again, Laura touched his arm, her voice soft and tender.

"Cabe, why don't you go shower and get into pajamas?"

"I don't wear pajamas."

Laura glanced at him exasperatedly. She was nervous enough about tonight, she didn't need to hear that. "Well, a robe then. I think I'll get Heather cleaned up before I run home to shower and dress."

Bathing the tiny-boned child was a taste of the sweet, maternal pleasure Laura so hungered for. But she begrudged every moment of her own shower and shampoo. Eagerness winged her feet as she ran lightly across the connecting lawns.

Preparing a meal in the manor's pretty blue and white kitchen was a pleasant task. KK lay on the rug, keeping a watchful eye on the frisky ginger kitten. Obviously resting easier, Cabe sat at the table with the newspaper while Heather bustled about laying place mats and napkins. Talk about domestic bliss! Laura thought. But the amusement in her thought was terribly weak. She could hardly restrain herself from hovering.

Chagrined to realize how emotionally involved she had become in a few short weeks, Laura wryly reminded herself she hadn't planned it. In any case, she'd have to be less than a woman to resist the milieu she found herself thrust into by a twist of fate.

Unbidden, she thought of another woman who could have been sharing all this and wonder pricked her. What had Michele done that was so terrible he had taken his daughter and walked out of the marriage?

Quickly Laura snapped off the unpleasant line of thought. It had no place in this cheerful kitchen. Although Cabe didn't say much, happy conversation filled the room with warmth.

The intimacy was bewitching to all its occupants. "I wish we could do this all the time," Heather confided.

Laura's heart wrenched. Quickly she glanced at Cabe's relaxed face. He hadn't heard the whispered confidence. "It is fun, isn't it!" she whispered back, then said crisply, "Supper's ready, Cabe, so put down the newspaper."

His eyes glinted, but he put it down.

Dolly's food sack had contained a honey-glazed ham, scalloped potatoes, broccoli and a lavish salad of red cherry and yellow plum tomatoes in buttery avocado halves. With fresh baked bread and homemade butter, they had a veritable feast.

"No thanks to me," Laura confessed.

"How do you live, anyway?" Cabe asked curiously. "If you don't cook, I mean."

"Oh, people feed me, kind of like a stray puppy."

Cabe laughed. But weariness caught up with him shortly after the meal ended and his mood became tense and edgy.

"Why don't you go on to bed, Cabe?" Laura suggested. "You need to rest."

"Why don't you let me decide what I need? Or at least decide my bedtime."

His harsh tone make her jump, but Laura knew how vulnerable he was feeling. Anger was merely a form of protective armor.

Her silence got to Cabe. "You're right, I do need my rest," he said gruffly.

She waited until Heather had kissed him good-night before reminding him that she'd have to wake him up at ten o'clock for his medicine.

Cabe hesitated. He could just ask her to place the tablets and a pitcher of water on his nightstand. Instead he nodded and continued on to his bedroom.

When he came out of the bathroom the sheets were turned back, serenely blue and inviting to his stiff-muscled frame. The faintest whiff of her sweet scent touched his nostrils. Inhaling deeper than necessary, he slid his nude body into bed and drew the satiny comforter up to his waist. It had been an emotionally taxing day and he felt exhausted. But sleep proved elusive. Sighing, he turned on his side and lay staring out the window.

The night was starless and the sea an endless dark void. The specks of light that were home-bound fishing boats seemed incredibly fragile. He felt an aching kinship with them. Closing his eyes again, he let his mind drift back through the day, to the senseless elation he had felt upon awakening.

His separation from Laura had given him ample time to reflect wisely upon their relationship. But he hadn't. He'd simply missed her, with raw little jolts of shock at how much.

Several other small shocks occurred during his absence. While in New York he had enjoyed looking up friends he hadn't seen since he and Michele split up. Walking into his office had suffused him with a professional pleasure he hadn't experienced in many months.

Reviving interests, a sense of dynamic energy, and guarded flickers of hope. After the afternoon with Laura, he couldn't help wondering if this was a new beginning.

"More like a case of you thinking like a fool," he muttered. Surely it was foolishness to entertain the notion that being with Laura could unravel his disordered tangle of emotions. She was still off limits.

Convincing himself of that would be a lot easier if he could forget what she wore beneath her clothes, Cabe mused. That glimpse of black silk on ivory-gold skin...

He must have dozed off, for her soft tap on his door startled him. When she came in his heart stopped completely before rocketing off on a thunderous new beat. The hallway fixture formed a golden halo of light over her head. Her hair was still damp from her shower and wispy tendrils wreathed her heart-shaped face. The alluring softness of a pale pink sweater and darker pink slacks outlined her curvaceous figure. His gaze traveled from her breasts to the sensuous peaks of her upper lip. He almost groaned as the hot weakness in the pit of his stomach arrowed downward. Hastily he adjusted the comforter about his thighs.

She came closer. "Time for your medicine, Cabe."

"You don't have to whisper. I'm awake." Cabe turned on his bedside lamp. His ankle was throbbing and he was glad to take the tablets. When she made as if to leave he stopped her with a quiet, "Sit down a minute?"

Hesitantly, Laura complied, her breath coming quicker at the intimacy of sitting on the edge of his bed with him in it, nude, as far as she could see. His chest was satin-smooth bronze in the lamp's light. Contrarily, his firm jaw and chin were covered with dark stubble. For a fleeting moment she gave in to the fantasy of imagining its roughness against her tender skin.

He folded his arms beneath his head. "You haven't been to bed yet?"

"No. I wasn't sleepy, just nicely tired. So I waited up."

Cabe shut his eyes to the echoing throb in another part of his body. "This was a stupid, avoidable accident," he stated. "I'm astonished that you haven't said 'I told you so.'"

Laura took a few seconds to steady her voice. His lashes cast sooty shadows over his strong cheekbones. His mouth looked so vulnerable she ached.

"I thought it, believe me."

"I'll bet you did," he murmured, chuckling. "Laura, if I haven't thanked you yet for all this fussing over me—"

"No thanks necessary. Anytime anyone we care about gets sick or hurt, he gets fussed over. Kind of like a reflex action, I guess," she said, her voice deepening as she struggled to resist the temptation he posed to her femaleness. It would be heaven to slip into that bed with him, to be caught close and held tight by those powerful arms. She could never get free once they imprisoned her. She wouldn't want to get free....

Blushing, she sprang to her feet. For goodness sake, Laura! she chastised herself. The man's injured and all you can think about is ravishing him!

She bent down and pressed a kiss into the taut skin of his cheek, much like she had done with Heather. "Go back to sleep now, Cabe. Good night."

Cabe's breath had fled him and for a scalding instant he was was totally incapable of speech. The soft kiss she had burned into his skin was all the more seductive for being so innocently given. Her perfumed warmth poured into him and he had to call upon every ounce of willpower he possessed to fight the fiery desire she ignited.

Huskily he bid her good night. Affection and need shuddered his hard body as she smiled and touched his hand before hurrying out the door. Gazing unseeing at the ceiling, he pondered the question that loomed large in his hazing mind. He knew the nature of his need well enough. But was it habitual affection that gripped his heart? Or something far more complex?

Wearily he sighed his confusion. The latter would require a corresponding lessening of negative emotions, and how was he going to figure that out?

"Good morning!" Dolly said brightly as Cabe followed the smell of morning coffee to the kitchen. "Laura left early to help Pearl set out the fresh supplies people are bringing in. Did you sleep well? How's that foot feel? Laura says it'll just be a couple of days until you're up and about again. Here, sit down here and I'll make you a good breakfast."

"Just toast and some of those strawberry preserves I bought yesterday, please," Cabe said, smiling. Evidently the chattering rush of words ran in the family. Her apron was pink and frilly today. "John Ed here, is he?"

"Yes," she blushed endearingly. "He says starting Monday he'll be working here full-time. Thank you, Cabe, that was really nice of you to hire him.

Cabe shrugged. "Nothing nice about it—taking care of this place properly is a full-time job. Tell me, does Laura make much money off this craft fair?" he asked idly.

"Not really. Once the artists collect their money, there's not that much left. But it's become sort of a tradition now, and besides, it makes Pearl feel important," she confided so puckishly he laughed.

"Is Laura doing all right financially?" he asked in the same, unpressing tone.

"We're getting along," Dolly said a little stiffly. "Once Pearl's pictures catch on, we'll do even better. I hear that people pay hundreds of dollars for art not half as good as hers. I wouldn't take any money for the one she did for me.

It's a precious treasure. Oh, you had some mail in your box. John Ed put it outside on the terrace where he thought you'd probably sit some today, it being a beautiful day and all.''

Her fluted voice was pleasant to his ears as Cabe ate his breakfast. Requesting that she prepare him a coffee tray, he hobbled out to the terrace and lowered himself into a chaise longue. Absently he rifled through his mail, his mind on Pearl's paintings. He hadn't really paid much attention to them. It wouldn't hurt to buy one or two.

Pearl and her paintings vanished from mind as he picked up a letter from Michele. Impassively he studied the blue-bordered envelope. Mailed from New York. Judging from the date, they had just missed each other.

He laughed with harsh humor—wouldn't that have been something, though! After two years of total separation to round a New York street corner and bump into his ex-wife.

Though the wording was stronger, Michele's letter was basically the same. His hard, silent laugh burst free again. The woman had gall, he'd give her that. But Heather was staying right here with him.

"Daddy? Watch me, Daddy!"

His daughter's cry jerked his head up. She was crouched on a tree limb at the side of the house. Having gained his attention she jumped to the ground, landing on her fanny with a soft "Oof!" She picked herself up, dusted off her jeans, and ran to him for some well-deserved praise.

The constriction in his chest compacted as she dashed into his arms. Holding her fragile form, Cabe felt the familiar surge of hostility sweep through him like spring floodwaters. Well, you got your answer to last night's question, he lauded himself bleakly. You're still just as bitter and angry as you were the day she left you.

"You're squishing me, Daddy."

"Sorry." He loosened his clasp.

"'At's okay. I'm going to play with KK now. I'll be right over there if you need me, Daddy," she assured him earnestly.

"Thanks, sweetheart." Sending her off with a love-pat on the bottom, Cabe closed his eyes until the wave of frustration had run its course. In its wake came an inexpressible sadness as he thought of a once-lovely dream and the part Heather would have played in it. She had been cheated of so much!

"Here's your coffee." Dolly was back. "Anything else I can do for you, Cabe?"

"No, thanks," he said gently. Handing her the mail, he requested she put it on his dresser.

Dolly went inside, her good heart troubled. What on earth had made that boy's eyes look like that? As she stacked his mail neatly on the dresser, the return address on Michele's letter caught her attention. So that's why, she thought. What did that woman have over him that could wipe the joy right out off his face?

Shaking her head, Dolly went on to the kitchen. She decided not to mention the incident to Laura.

"Everything went fine, honey," she assured her niece that evening. "Cabe's been a little quiet, but I guess that's only natural. I doubt he's the type of man to enjoy just laying about."

Laura doubted it, too. But if he expected her to politely put up with a grouch, he was in for a surprise. She was tired and in need of a good night's sleep, and felt a bit grumpy herself. Assessingly, she stuck her head inside the den door. His greeting was friendly, if a little terse.

Relieved, she came on in. Heather was ensconced in her beanbag chair with KK, the ginger kitten, and a children's puppet show. They were having pizza for dinner, she said. Laura thought that a wonderful idea.

"I haven't ordered it yet," Cabe said, frowning as she sank down on the ottoman and worked her neck. "Stiff?"

"Ah, yeah, stiff. And tired. Seems like I was wanted in a dozen places at once every time I turned around today," she sighed, massaging her shoulders. "Your ankle looks much better—swelling's gone down a lot. How's the pain?"

"Bearable. Come here, let me do that," he ordered.

Having not the slightest desire to defy him, Laura sat down on the edge of his chair with her back to him. Long, hard fingers rolled over her shoulders, working and massaging, digging deep and releasing. Her head dropped limply forward as a heavenly sensation of tingling warmth began to dissolve points of tension. Thoughts drifted through her mind, of warmed oil and naked skin and those masterful hands. Pulling herself back to reality, she nearly moaned aloud with the small taste of bliss he was giving her.

"Have you ever thought about selling the store?" he asked abruptly. "Its location should give your property substantial value."

"I've had offers," she conceded, drawing away a little. "But that's been Richards's property for over a century and I wouldn't think of selling it."

They argued without rancor, Cabe pointing out that that sentiment was all well and good, but not when it prohibited the practicality of selling a ridiculously unprofitable business, and Laura retorting that she preferred sentiment over cold-blooded practicality anytime.

Yielding his point, he suggested a loan, knowing it was wasted words by the lift of her chin. "Thank you, Cabe," she said, slipping her hands over his. "It's really sweet of you to worry about me, but I'm doing okay."

He shrugged and dropped it. "I've decided to go to Raleigh with Heather, some business to attend to. Besides, it wouldn't hurt to have my regular doctor check out this leg. I've already notified the pilot and we'll be leaving early in the morning. I'll be back Wednesday or Thursday."

He removed his hands from her shoulders. Feeling the loss keenly, she stood up and straightened her blouse. "Would you like me to drive you to the airport?"

"John Ed's already volunteered."

"You should feel right at home in that old pickup of his," she quipped, and he laughed briefly.

While he ordered their pizza, Laura went home for a restorative shower. She dressed in a sapphire-blue lounging outfit styled on the order of harem pants and a wrap blouse that tied at one side of her waist. With it she wore high heels. Cabe whistled when she came in, and Heather thought she looked "beautifuller than a movie star."

Although Laura relished Cabe's playful reaction, her feminine intuition was as sharp as ever where he was concerned. Behind his bland mask he was tense and oddly wary. She wondered about the cause, but didn't question. Intuition also told her that he had no intention of confiding in her. Vowing to keep a tight rein on her curiosity, she invited Heather to help prepare a tray of raw vegetables and pickles to go with the pizza.

The evening was much like the last one. Once Heather was bathed and in pajamas, they watched television and sipped fruity red wine. Candlewick flames danced on the hearth. At dusk, river fog began rolling in to shrink their world to this cozy, softly-lit room. Laura's romantic heart was helpless to resist the lovely illusion of closeness.

Cabe, too, appeared more relaxed and at ease with himself. Reacting to the sweet, bemused smile playing about his mouth, Laura flung caution to the winds and joyously gave herself up to the pleasure of simply being with him.

Heather's bedtime came, though she didn't think so. Cabe tried persuasion. It didn't work, and he had to resort to a reprimand, which led to tears and then to making up and profuse explanations of why he had to discipline her.

What a softy he is, Laura thought fondly. Suspecting that the child was going to fall asleep in her father's lap and would have to be carried to bed, she went into the luscious strawberry and cream bedroom across the hall and turned down the eyelet-trimmed coverlet.

When she returned, Cabe's dark head rested against the pale silk of his drowsy daughter's hair. "She needs a little extra cuddling tonight," he said, daring Laura to say differently.

"A shame you don't have a rocking chair," she murmured. "Through with the TV?" He nodded. She turned it off, then kicked off her shoes and curled up on the couch. A tiny smile tilted her lips as she caught his gaze on her again.

The clock ticked hypnotically. Her eyelids grew heavy. Perhaps because she was so weary, or perhaps just because she felt unusually fragile tonight, Laura was powerless to combat the intense longing that sliced through her. This man, this child, this house; my heart's desire, she thought dreamily. All that's missing is the cradle beside our hearth.

The wind picked up a handful of rain and flung it against the windows. Laura jerked upright with a little frisson of alarm. She was fully aware what a dangerous fantasy she was weaving.

But that didn't make it any less seductive.

Ten

Every diversion Laura came up with the night before her
aunt's surgery, was dully rejected. Pearl wrung her hands
and apologized for being so apathetic. "It's just that I won't
even be able to celebrate my birthday on Tuesday—maybe
not at all. Well, it's a possibility," she defended against
Dolly's hard sigh.

An echoing sigh came from Laura. Her aunt's fearful
anxiety was hard on the heart. "Aunt Pearl, we may have a
late birthday celebration, but we will have one, believe me.
Please don't go getting yourself all worked up about tomorrow. The doctor told you there's nothing to fear, that
it'll all be done in his office, with you so sedated you won't
feel a thing. And you know I'll be right there with you."

"Mary Laura, honey," Pearl said nervously, "no of-
fense, but Dolly and me, we go back a long ways, you
know? I can't do this without her there beside me. You will
be there, won't you, Dolly?"

"I don't know, Pearl," Dolly replied slowly. "I been thinking on it, but . . . well, you know I can't drive, and you sure won't be able to get us home. Somebody has to keep store, and we can't go expecting John Ed to drop everything and help us out every time there's a problem." Pride crept into her troubled tone. "He's got his own job now."

Pearl looked crushed, and Laura couldn't stand it. In the end she locked up the store and hung a hand-printed Closed for Pearl's Surgery sign on the door. Pearl wore her good linen-blend skirt and blouse, and her finest underwear. "In case I die in the chair," she told Dolly.

"Oh, shoot, Pearl, you're not going to die in any dental chair!" Dolly snorted. "When you go it'll be in a blaze of glory. Probably with half a dozen of your swains in attendance," she added dryly.

Pearl looked pleased at that.

The handsome young periodontist charmed her despite her suspicions of what he did to people in closed little surgical rooms. Laura liked him, too, and took her mind off what he did by speculating on what beautiful babies those blond good looks would produce. Green eyes, of course, curly hair, dark, with auburn highlights. She smiled wryly; it wasn't the good doctor's genes she was thinking of.

Dolly was pacing. Laura advised her to sit down and read a magazine, there was absolutely no reason to worry. Nonetheless, she didn't draw an easy breath until Pearl was wheeled into the waiting area and pronounced fine.

Laura paid the bill without batting an eyelash. Handing over the check, however, imbued her with a dull sense of defeat as she calculated upcoming expenses. It was taking more and more effort to conceal her troubled spirits.

Checking on Pearl each morning evoked another, more primitive worry. The snap was gone from her eyes. Even her bright curls lay limp around her small head. "She looks so old and frail," Dolly fretted.

"She's neither old nor frail. Pearl's as strong as an ox, you know that. Soon as the trauma of surgery wears off, she'll be back to her old self,'' Laura asserted firmly, but a mild depression rode her shoulders. The only note of cheer she could find was the pleasure Pearl derived from the flowers Cabe had sent her by special air messenger, the most outrageous, most exotic flower arrangement anyone had ever seen. It had arrived Tuesday evening, along with the latest SciFi Book of the Month selection and a small gold charm for her bracelet, in the form of a conceptual alien spaceship that delighted her heart.

Pearl's eyes were enormous. "It's from Cabe?"

"Who else?" Laura said, chuckling to screen the catch in her voice. Mixed with her various concerns was an unrelenting yearning for Cabe's presence. Not just his presence, she acknowledged forthrightly. Her physical needs were fully as strong. She had to actively remind herself that he had only kissed her twice. The dull, relentless ache afflicting her soft body was very similar to that of a woman eagerly awaiting a sexual reunion with her lover.

Some imagination, Mary Laura, she mocked her restive self. But when he walked into the store Thursday afternoon, Laura was ill-prepared for the rushing gladness of simply seeing him again. Her smile was uncontainable. "Well, hello, neighbor! You're back on the cane," she observed brightly. "Your ankle's on the mend, then?"

"Yes, no permanent damage to the ankle or leg." His gaze raced over her, then moved on to her aunt without changing expression.

Pearl sat in the old wicker rocker with an afghan tucked around her legs. She waved away her effusive thanks for her birthday presents. His inquiry about her health, followed by a compliment on how good she was looking, perked up her wan smile considerably.

"She has to be getting better," Laura said. "Tell him why, Aunt Pearl."

Prettily confused, Pearl fiddled with her hair. "It's not that much, really. I had a telephone call just a few minutes ago—in fact, I haven't even had a chance to tell Dolly yet, but it was a reporter from the newspaper, requesting an interview." Color flared in her pallid cheeks. "Can you believe that? They want to interview me. *Me*, Dolly!"

"What on earth for?" Dolly asked, incredulous.

"An article about my paintings—local artist and all that," Pearl said, preening a little. She frowned. "But how'd they find out about me, I wonder?"

"Probably from one of those craft-show flyers," Laura said, though secretly she doubted it. Much to Pearl's delight, Cabe was making teasing comments about the celebrity in their midst and displaying a flattering interest in her opinions on the book he had sent her.

He could be so charming, Laura thought. She avoided looking at Dolly, whose eyes were saying the same thing and more. No sooner had he walked out the door than she nudged Pearl knowingly. "See? The first place he comes to when he gets back to town is here," she said, grinning slyly at Laura, who serenely ignored her.

Undaunted, at closing time Dolly brought out half a freshly baked chocolate-meringue pie, Cabe's favorite, and requested that Laura give it to him.

"If I see him, Aunt Dolly," Laura agreed mildly.

Nevertheless, there was a spring in Laura's step as she walked out into the balmy gold and blue evening. She was almost sure Cabe would call. Holding the enticing pie out of KK's leaping reach, she deposited it on the kitchen table and hurried to check her answering machine. Although she had several messages, his was not among them.

At seven-fifteen he still hadn't called. I'm acting like a teenager waiting for the telephone to ring, Laura thought, poignantly amused. Apparently the need to feel wanted was the same at any age. She cut a sliver of the pie for KK, who was a fiend for chocolate, then closed the cardboard box.

Covered or not, it was tempting reason to follow her heart's urging. Wondering, exasperatedly, why she had even tried to resist it, Laura picked up her very good reason and went to deliver it.

She chose the terrace door. As was the local custom among good neighbors, she tapped, waited, then opened it a crack and called, "Anybody home?"

"In the bedroom. Come sit and talk to me while I finish dressing," Cabe called back. "Hey, Sunshine!" he said breezily as she peered around the edge of his open bedroom door.

Laura's dimples flickered annoyedly as she coupled the use of her old nickname with the careless invitation to enter his private quarters. He was regressing her to a girl again.

Clad in trim black slacks and a crisp white shirt, Cabe stood in profile at his dressing-room mirror brushing his damp hair. "To what do I owe the pleasure of this visit?" he asked indulgently.

"Aunt Dolly sent you half a chocolate pie," Laura replied. Her knees were trembling. She sat down on the foot of his bed. "I put it in the refrigerator for you."

"I thank both you and Aunt Dolly." He grinned at her.

"You're welcome, I'm sure," Laura tossed back. Her power of speech faltered as he began splashing on after-shave. The spicy scent seem to surround her. Swallowing, she clasped her hands.

"I was also looking for a dinner date tonight. You available?"

"I've already got a dinner date tonight. Sorry," Cabe said, deliberately succinct.

"Oh." She leaned back on her hands. "In that case I withdraw the invitation."

Her tone was unperturbed, but Cabe saw her eyes before those extravagant dark lashes shuttered them. Pivoting, he jerked down a red silk tie. "Business."

"What?"

"It's a business dinner with the local banker and the owners of that tract of land Cord and I are buying."

Laura sat up. "Then you've definitely decided to buy it? What will you do with it?"

"Develop part of it. Summer homes, mostly. The other part will be set aside as a bird sanctuary, courtesy of Heather Ann McClain and Jason Cordoba Hunter."

"Oh, Cabe, that's wonderful," she said huskily.

He rolled the tie under his collar, doing a bad job of it. "I think so. Anyway, I'll be traveling most of next week trying to correlate all my business interests. Noel will be in charge of the New York offices," he said, referring to the younger brother he had taken into the firm years ago. "I'll handle things at this end."

Laura's "Oh!" had two syllables and came out on a trembly breath. She was delighted by his strengthening ties with the community, and thrilled by this dynamic new air of vibrancy. Swinging a foot nonchalantly, she asked, "Then you'll establish an office in Raleigh?"

"Maybe later. Right now I'll run things from here, from the computer-communications room I'm having installed in that downstairs study. I'll be in instantaneous touch with New York, Hunter Enterprises, local employees—all with just a touch of a button!"

"You really are excited about this, aren't you," Laura said, her eyes soft.

"Yeah. I guess I am."

The smile he gave her was irresistibly warm and boyish. Succumbing to it, Laura got up and went to him. He was still struggling with his tie. "Here, let me have a try," she murmured, and lifted her arms to assist him.

Cabe's defenses flooded him with such absurdly strong wariness he felt embarrassed. You'd think she was a full grown lioness coming at you, he mocked his instant reaction. But he had returned feeling strong and vigorous, full of fresh resolve to keep dangerous man-women elements out of their cherished friendship. That's why he'd invited her to his room in the first place, to prove to himself that he could. Gingerly, he let himself relax. What she was doing seemed harmless enough. How many other women had fixed his tie for him?

"How could I survive without you to help me?" he kidded her, laughing as she made a face at him just like she used to do. It felt perfectly natural to link his fingers loosely at the back of her waist.

But that was the trouble with Laura. Everything came so naturally that she slipped under his guard before he realized he'd even lowered it.

The first measured beats of a primitive drum began pounding in his blood as she stepped closer. Her slim fingers were satiny cool against his throat as she undid the crooked tie. Scant inches separated his needful maleness from the alluring femininity just below his hands. Her fragrant warmth bridged the tiny distance and surged into him through every dilating pore.

She raised her arms higher to reinsert the length of fabric under his collar. Cabe went rigid, forgetting even the basics of breathing as their thighs touched. Her breasts pressed against his chest with such tantalizingly light pressure that he felt aflame from the neck down. Nearly starved for air, he sucked in a breath that brought her questioning gaze to his.

Her eyes took on a sensuous gleam. She didn't look away and he could not. The heart-jolting electricity flowing from her body to his provoked a silent groan. His mind skittered wildly, fighting the restraints he had set for himself. Staggered by how desperately he wanted to take her, Cabe looked impatiently at his watch.

She glanced up at him, a half smile on her face. "There, that's better," she murmured, straightening the perfectly knotted tie.

"Much better. Hand me that jacket hanging on the chair? Thanks," he said as she held it for him.

His body so tense he felt breakable, Cabe draped an arm around her shoulders and casually began walking her to the den. Triumph flickered in his green eyes. He had resisted the irresistible. Control. It was always there in a pinch.

"Oh, here," he remembered as they passed a bow-bedecked box sitting on a table. "I saw this in a New York shop window and thought it looked like something you might like."

Wide-eyed, Laura regarded the box, then his face. "A present?"

"Why not?" Cabe retorted. "I like to give presents. Anyway, it's just a trinket, Sunshine."

"It is not just a trinket," she murmured. The elegant crystal figurine, a fawn and doe poised as if testing the wind, bore a famous name. "Oh, Cabe, it's utterly exquisite. Thank you."

"You're welcome." Cabe laughed, enjoying the warmth of giving, especially to her. "About your suggestion concerning a housekeeper," he remarked, "you really think Dolly would be interested?"

Pleased surprise flooded her eyes. "Yes, I think so! But why have you changed your mind?"

"Because of you—why else? You made it sound like only an ogre would deprive a child of summer vacation," he said.

"If the shoe fits..." she murmured. "When would you need Aunt Dolly? Not right away, I hope—she wouldn't even consider it until Pearl's all well."

"No, of course not." He opened the terrace door and stepped outside with her. "Heather's not out of school until the end of the month."

"That should work out. Another week or so and Pearl will be back to her old self. I'll talk to Aunt Dolly for you. I hope you enjoy your evening, Cabe." Laura shaded her eyes to gaze at the cloud-banked horizon. "If my lights are still on when you come in and you feel like it, come on over and we'll talk, maybe have a game of chess. Since I've been having a little trouble sleeping lately," she said with a faint smile for her understatement, "I'd welcome some company."

Cabe smiled. There he stood, cool as a cucumber, murmuring a noncommittal something about the expected late ness of his return while his brain worked feverishly to detect a hint of erotic overtones in her invitation.

His speculations were idiotically absorbing. Dusk slipped unnoticed into lightning-streaked darkness. An excellent meal with interesting dinner guests passed into vague recall as arguments and counter-arguments besieged his mind. He settled the dispute with a harsh reminder that the nature of her invitation didn't matter; nothing had changed. Sexual involvement with Laura would still be a greedy taking without giving anything in return, because he had nothing to give. He was still empty inside, his heart still dead to love.

But his green eyes gleamed as he left the expensive hush of the restaurant. The smoldering heat of desire pulsed unrelentingly through his veins.

In the near distance, thunder rumbled. The moon wove in and out of tattered clouds. Pacing the length of her small patio, Laura methodically pulled a brush through her freshly washed hair. Behind her the stereo spun out a soft melody and she timed the movements to its muted beat, hoping that it would ultimately prove soothing. But nothing seemed to work tonight, not even the boat ride she had taken earlier. Usually a panacea for her restive spirit, the wild, headlong dash across an empty sea had stimulated rather than calmed.

Even KK's bark had grated on her nerves. She had shut him in the guest bedroom, where apparently he'd fallen asleep. Nothing broke the pre-storm hush except for the music welling through the screened glass doors.

She froze in midstep as the sound of a motor blended into the pulsing refrain. Cabe's car lights flashed through the trees to her right. No house lights appeared. Was he coming to visit her?

So acutely did she listen for his footsteps that when she heard them, Laura wasn't certain if it was Cabe, or the pounding rush of blood in her ears. A tall, dark shadow moving through a silvered forest, he crossed the side lawn

and came around to the patio where she waited. At the sight
of him, longing swelled through her body.

Cabe's voice had gotten lost, too. His mind, though, was
still working in a disjointed sort of way. I knew it was crazy,
he thought. That sweet face and bewitching mouth. But I
was too keyed up to go to bed so I figured I'd just stroll over
and talk awhile. That's all, just talk. What arrogance. The
proud thrust of her breasts. I haven't touched them. Those
long, silken legs. I should turn around and go back, now,
while I can. But his feet were flagrantly disobedient to
mental commands. She was smiling at him, that dusky cloud
of hair tumbling down and around her naked shoulders, lips
parted, her tongue darting out as if catching the taste of
him, and liking it. Lord, McClain, don't have these kinds of
thoughts!

"Hi," she said.

"Hello." Was that rusty voice his? But even the wind's
against me, he thought. It licked at her short dress, teasing
the fragile ties that held it up at the shoulders, molding the
thin fabric against her body and making it killingly evident
that she wore nothing else. He stared at her, desperately
seeking innocence. Glimpsed through enchanting dark
lashes, her eyes were sultry, aware. This sensuous woman,
he reflected wonderingly. How could I have ever thought it
possible to keep her a girl?

"You're lovely, Laura," he said, speaking almost ab-
stractedly. "The loveliest thing I've ever seen."

"Thank you." Laura felt giddy with excitement, drunk on
it. The wild, black night was as potent a seduction of her
senses as the man who watched her every move.

He smiled, a gentle, sexy smile. Her lips opened wider, her
breath hurrying between them. It was frightening to experience this swirling depth of feeling. But she couldn't retreat. Longing was too weak a word now. She craved him.
I'm not afraid, she thought.

"Let's go inside, Cabe..." She laughed and caught at her
hair. "Before I blow away!"

Cabe shook his head once. Just smelling her sweet woman scent had him hard and throbbing. He couldn't come in. He wouldn't come in.

"Close the glass door behind you," she said, and he watched himself step inside and close it.

He loosened his tie and she helped him out of his jacket. Both items were tossed on a nearby chair. Facing him, she flung back her hair. The curl that wound itself around his fingers was still damp, like moist satin.

"Do you..." Laura coughed, touched her throat. "Want to try that chess game now?"

Her words, at first merely scattered sounds, condensed and assumed meaning. Acting on some vague hope of holding back the tide of desire, Cabe grasped her shoulders, and knew the instant he did so that he'd made another mistake. Contact with her warm, silken flesh ignited a blazing wildfire. All the reasons why they should not make love burned away like river mist on a July morning.

"No. It's you I want," he said thickly. "I don't want to, but I do." His hooded gaze met hers and hungrily locked. "Tell me."

She licked her lips. "You know."

"Yes." He ran his hands down her back to the sensuous curves that had tormented his fingers many a night. "Yes." They gripped the soft mounds and strained her to him. With ravishing intent, she rubbed against him until he groaned and caught her mouth in a kiss that was like no other.

How long he drank of her intoxicating honey he didn't know. At length, stunned with delight, he drew back, shuddering. The sweet, hot weakness sucked at him, simultaneously turning his legs to jelly while giving him the strength of ten men. Slipping an arm under her thighs, he swept her up to his chest.

Her head fell back. The silken mane of hair cascaded down his forearm. She laughed, rich and voluptuous and feminine. It was magic. In his mind he didn't limp or stumble along. He walked tall and proud, he strode like a conqueror. With savage male exhilaration he carried her down the hall to her bedroom.

Rather than lowering her, he let her slide down his body and thought for a moment that he would shatter into a million pieces. Blindly he groped for the tiny straps on her shoulders. With but a gentle pull they came untied and the supple garment slithered down her body to fall in a turquoise pool around her feet.

"Ah, Laura," he said in a sigh that mingled with the wind keening outside their windows. She was breathtaking. Curving in, flaring out, a living ivory sculpture. Her breasts were sheer perfection. Their ripe fullness filled the cupped hollows of his palms. He brought them to his mouth and found them ambrosial, the dusky aureoles wine on the lips, the rosy nipples fragrantly sweet and delicate, like tiny wild strawberries on the tongue. He wanted to devour her.

Laura went limp against him. She felt weightless, afloat on rivers of sensation. When he took her inside the wet silkiness of his mouth, she moaned again and pulled demandingly at his shirt.

Feverishly eager to please her, Cabe stripped off his garments and felt his whole system respond as she ran a fingertip from his chest to the line of hair that flowed down his flat belly. She stopped there, as if uncertain. Slowly her eyes met his. In their velvety depths he saw the exquisite shyness so at odds with her frank sexuality. Tenderness rushed to his head. He needed to comfort and protect, to stand like a brave white knight between her and harm. More than anything, he needed her. Without a word he gathered her in and kissed her with the fierce, raw urgency of passion careening out of control.

For Laura, the next few moments were a dazzling kaleidoscope of sensations and impressions. Rain sluiced against the window as he pressed her down into the coolness of linen and the yielding of the pillows he slid under her hips. A whip-crack of lightning and the tom-tom beat of her heart ... or was it his? The feel of his hands on her, his fingers stitching molten threads across her quivering flesh, binding her to him, a willing captive, the soft inferno of his breath searing intimate flesh. Suddenly she knew, with implacable surety, that she would never want another man's hands touching her like this, would never want another man. There was only him. *Take care, Laura.*

Then even that cautioning thought fled. His caresses roughened and she thrilled to this dark, demanding side of his nature. As he lowered himself to her, the air burst through her lips in rapturous shock. He filled her, slowly, then faster. She gasped again. He stopped, waited. "Laura?"

Red stars danced beneath her lashes so tightly did she shut her eyes to contain the glory. He was terrifyingly the dominant male. She loved it, loved feeling so deliciously small and fragile beneath the muscled power of him, knowing she could control and guide that potent power with just a word, a touch. She raised her lashes and found him gazing down at her, his eyes brilliant, intense, his teeth clenched as he restrained himself.

"Yes, oh yes, oh yes..." She drew his head down, and burned the sensuous little chant into his lips as he took her higher, ever higher. Poised on the brink of ecstasy, Cabe struggled mightily to resist the excitement bombarding his system. Then her lips slid across his face to his ear to issue a stunningly erotic command. A moment later ecstasy exploded through them like a chain of starbursts.

Luxuriously spent, they held each other for a timeless interlude. In slow motion, Cabe lifted his head to look at the woman who lay in the crook of his arm with a hand curled palm-up on his chest, her lashes downcast, that half smile on her lips. One peach-gold shoulder was completely hidden under a fall of soft brown hair. With a ragged inner sigh, he relinquished his claim on euphoria. The bitter tug of war between the heaven and hell of his present situation had already started.

It would be funny if it didn't hurt so much, he thought with biting self-mockery. Going along smug as hell, the man in control, when all the time the only thing you were master of was fooling yourself. And who pays for your arrogant delusions?

Laura.

She stirred at his long release of breath. "What?"

"Laura, I..." He pinched the bridge of his nose. *No lies.*

She sighed. "Never mind, I know. Instead of lying here marveling about how glorious this was, you're worrying about future complications." She tipped back her head to see his face. "Frankly, I think you're quite wonderful for that. Because your concern is for me, not yourself. You're afraid I might get hurt, might be left bitter, might even get pregnant—"

Cabe's short laugh burst out of him. If only pregnancy was a viable concern! He opened his mouth and found her fingertips across it.

"Hush and let me finish. I'm not making light of your fears, they'd be very real under different circumstances. But not under these. I've wanted you since that first day, wanted to have you in my bed, knew perfectly well I eventually would, and felt marvelous about it. Well, actually, I didn't start feeling marvelous about it until a little later when I stopped being embarrassed about it...." She laughed and blushed. "But anyway you get my point. So take that worried look off your face, please? I'm all grown up now—"

"Are you?"

"Yes. A woman now." Saucy mischief lit her dark eyes. "A greedy woman."

An odd little smile flitted across his mouth, then was gone. "You are, hmm?"

Not knowing what to make of it, she laughed and answered huskily, "Oh yes. Very greedy." A cannonade of thunder shook the small cottage. She lowered her head until their breaths mingled. Her eyes glittered. She wet her lips. "I don't want to talk anymore. Do you?"

"No. Come here."

It rained all day Friday and through much of the night. Opening her eyes to Saturday's bright sunlight, Laura flung a hand across the bed, then sighed deeply at her automatic reach for the man in whose arms she had fallen asleep. She would have loved waking up to him, but as before, she woke alone. Well, you can't have everything, she told herself. And just why not? an answering inner voice demanded to know.

Her laugh evolved into a troubled sigh as she realized how much of herself she had given Cabe during their blissful interlude. But he had lowered his guard with her only fractionally. No promises were spoken, not a single word of love. She realized something else. She could not give up this wild rapture even if she wanted to. He was a potent drug, and she was addicted.

She shrugged, annoyed at the trickle of unease. She knew their relationship was coming closer and closer to the kind of commitment that could bind two hearts together. She was fairly certain that Cabe knew it, too. Nothing was said, but words weren't necessary. Remembering the previous night's pleasure of dancing and dining in vibrant awareness of the delight to follow restored her small loss of confidence. Feeling wonderfully strong and invincible, Laura rose up on her knees and opened the window to the beautiful, storm-washed morning.

Wild roses perfumed the air. A frisky wind white-capped the river and hung scraps of cloud out to dry. Languidly she glanced at the clock and jumped out of bed with an exasperated groan. This was her second day in a row to oversleep and she had a suspicion that such uncharacteristic behavior would not be ignored.

She was right. "If it don't be all what a little extra sleep will do for a woman's complexion!" Dolly marveled to Pearl as their radiant niece sauntered into the store forty-five minutes past opening time. Her blue eyes innocent as a cream-stealing kitten's, she asked Laura blandly, "You and Cabe getting along a little better lately, honey?"

"Now, Dolly, behave," Pearl admonished. "Bite your tongue if you have to, but no more sly questions, you hear? Some things aren't meant to be exposed to the glarin' light of curiosity."

"Thank you, Aunt Pearl," Laura crooned, but her smile held a sea of gratitude. Her relationship with Cabe was too exquisitely personal to bandy about with anyone.

"You're welcome, love. Where is that boy today?"

"Doing something with Heather, I suppose. He was picking her up at the airport at eleven."

Though Laura spoke carelessly, by late afternoon she was counting minutes. Business was light, but steady. Otherwise she would have closed early, so keen was her desire to be with them.

Heather was in her backyard feuding with KK over possession of his little red ball when she got home. "Hi, you two! Where's your father?" she asked casually.

"He's showering." With a child's quicksilver change of mood, Heather forgot about the ball and ran to Laura, saying excitedly, "Miss Richards, do you know what? Only one more week of school! Daddy says come next Saturday I'll be here to stay and we'll all be good, good friends!"

Laura caught her breath in soft delight as two small arms wrapped around her hips in a tight hug. Tenderly she stroked the flaxen head. "You bet we will," she agreed. "But only if you call me Laura. Come, let's sit down on my fairy seat and talk. Good friends should know all about each other, don't you think? I know your favorite food and TV show, but tell me some of the other things you like best," she requested as they sat down on a slab of moss-ringed log. "Like who your favorite people are."

"Daddy. And Aunt Susan and Uncle Pete. Aunt Juliet and Uncle Cord." Green eyes smiled at her. "And you."

Laura blinked. "Thank you. But what about your mommy?"

"I don't know her. Just her picture. She sent me a Christmas present and a big white Easter bunny, but . . ." A tiny lift of shoulders completed the sentence.

"Would you like to know her?"

"I don't know. I might," Heather replied cautiously. "She wants to take me somewhere—I forget where—for two weeks in August. But Daddy said no, she didn't deserve me."

"Your daddy told you that?"

"No, I heard him fighting with her on the phone and so he had to tell me what about and that she didn't, so I couldn't."

Unraveling that, Laura said expressionlessly, "I see. But if you could, would you like to spend some time with your mother, get to know her?"

"Maybe. I don't know. All my other friends gots mommies. Some are diborced, but they still go places together." After that mispronunciation, Heather jumped up and grabbed the red ball. Obviously she was through with the subject.

Laura wasn't.

"What kind of relationship does Heather have with her mother?" she asked Cabe later than evening.

Cabe stared at her, irritation mingling with his surprise. Laura ruefully admitted she couldn't blame him. They had just returned from a wonderfully old-fashioned date, dinner at a drive-in café, then a movie and popcorn, topped off by a walk along the waterfront holding hands and kissing often. Now they were relaxing on her sofa enjoying a nightcap and the delicious anticipation of lovemaking—and up pops *this*.

"None to speak of," he said evenly. "And that's the way I intend to keep it, so let's not get into whatever's on your mind."

Laura was not one to heed notes of warning when she cared about someone. "You're on my mind, Cabe, you and a lovely little girl who doesn't know her mother except through presents. Why?'' she pressed softly.

"Because that's the way I want it, that's why."

The defensive arrogance in his reply stirred Laura, and angered her. "Whether or not it's best for Heather? And what about Michele?" she snapped, feeling an intense empathy with the woman who had not only lost her husband, but all contact with her child. "Heather told me about overhearing your fight with her. Frankly, I don't understand that, either. What's so outrageous about a mother wanting to spend two weeks with her only child?"

He tensed, his jaw working. "Nothing, if Michele were her mother. But all she did was give birth to Heather. A biological accident, you might say," he added with acrid humor. "Then she walked out of her life without a backward glance."

Confused, Laura said, "*She* walked out? But I thought—"

"I know what you thought." Cabe laughed harshly. "But the truth is, Michele left me, not the other way around." He downed the rest of his drink, wincing as the fiery liquid gouged a path down his throat. "Seems that when you switch priorities from family to career," he drawled, "a husband and baby are just so much excess baggage. So you dump them."

Laura's breath bunched up, then flew away as she realized fully what he was saying. Her first thought was that Michele was an utter fool. Her second was a violent need to strike out at the one responsible for the pain in Cabe's eyes. The one she acted on was a reminder that the woman was still Heather's mother.

"Cabe, I understand what you went through, even why you still feel so angry about it—"

"Do you?" He smiled. "I think not."

"Maybe not exactly, but I—I can imagine," she said, shaken by that bitter twist of lips. "But you have to forgive and forget, Cabe—"

"I don't have to do anything." Cabe set down his glass with a sharp little *crack* of sound. "I have complete, unrestricted custody of my daughter and that includes deciding what is and what is not best for her without interference from anyone." His voice was deadly quiet. "Now I think we'd better just drop this."

Laura thought so, too. But there was Heather. "There are still two facts that won't change regardless of what you do or do not decide," she plowed on. "Michele is still Heather's mother. And having custody doesn't give you the right to stop her from seeing her child."

"Maybe not, but I'll tell you what does give me that right. It's been over two years since that woman walked out on us and not once—not once—has she displayed an ounce of concern about what happened to her adored child." Cabe stood up and jammed his hands into his pockets. His tightly controlled voice gave hint of the enormous anger building up in him. "Have you any idea how it feels to try to explain to a two-year-old why Mommy's not coming home tonight? Or tomorrow night or next month or..." He turned to the window. "Forgive and forget? What she did to me, maybe—hell, that's no big deal—but not what she did to Heather."

"And what about you, Cabe?" Laura put in softly, "what about when *you* walked out on Heather? Or was going off to Brazil different?"

She had struck a raw nerve. Cabe wheeled on her, his eyes hard and brilliant. "You're damned right it was different. My going away was a matter of sheer self-preservation. Hers was self-centered gratification taken with total disregard for the cost to others. But now she's got it all, the career, the prestige, the media acclaim. Now she wants to play Mommy again."

"Cabe, don't," Laura said in a hurting whisper. She ached for his past anguish. But it was the past. "Don't hate her for that, don't hold onto all this bitterness, this rage. In the end it'll destroy the very things people love most about you, your warmth, your tenderness, even your ability to care. What occurred between you and Michele is history. Don't let it keep eating at you."

Standing, she went to him and tentatively touched his arm. "Let go of the past and get on with your life. It's out there, Cabe, waiting for you, all the love and joy and happiness a man could ever need—"

"Oh, stop it, Laura!" Cabe's control snapped as all the powerful forces churning inside him came to an explosive head and burst free in a blast of fury. "Stop being Little-Miss-Sweetness-and-Light, Everything's-Going-To-Come-Out-All-Right! Because it *doesn't* always come out all right, for every happy ending there's a thousand unhappy ones! You're living proof of that." Forgetful of his strength, he gripped her shoulders, his soft, icy voice much worse than a shout. "And stow the advice, too. I don't need anyone meddling in my private life. How I raise my daughter is none of your business."

She winced. "Cabe, that hurts."

Cabe thought she meant his grip. Confusion filled his green eyes. His hands dropped, leaden weights. "I'm sorry," he blurted. An instant later the door slammed behind him.

Laura was too stunned to call after him. Moving as if very tired, she walked to the bedroom they had shared for a few rapturous hours last night. Thoughts and images swirled through her mind. His eyes, so confused, so vulnerable. The savage outburst of emotion. His passionate anger. Michele. Beautiful, alluring. Fascinating. How he must have loved her, to feel with such intensity after all this time.

Or had he simply not gotten over her yet?

"No, that's not it." Startled at the sound of her raw voice, she lay down on the bed and pulled the covers up to her chin. Why was he so hostile, then?

KK's impatient barking and loving licks of tongue jarred Laura awake. Blinking at the sunlight, she focused her gaze

on the clock. After ten. Her mouth thinned with distaste as
she pushed back the quilt and sat up. No wonder she felt so
grubby—she had slept in her clothes! Making a face, she
stripped off the rumpled attire and headed for the shower.
At length, redressed in cut-off jeans, sneakers, and a blue
and white checked shirt, she put KK in his fenced run and
started toward the pier. Hearing her name, she paused, a
lump mushrooming in her throat as she spied the source of
the sound. Cabe and Heather were in the pool. He eased
over the blue-tiled rim and to his feet, then removed his
daughter to a lawn chair. "Stay here," she heard him tell
Heather.

He wore the same slick white trunks as before. Only this
time, Laura's body reminded her sharply, she knew how far
down his tan line went, and the terminus for that finger-
enticing arrow of hair bisecting his flat belly. She felt too
hot, too giddy, too everything.

"Laura." His gaze flickered downward. Her cut-offs were
old, the hems had unraveled to soft fringes just below the
junction of her thighs. "Going fishing?"

Laura smiled, but she was wary. Last night had hurt.
"Yes, with Pearl and Dolly and John Ed. We take him along
to help with unhooking our catch. In these waters you never
know what's going to be on the other end of the line and
none of us fancy fooling around with a sand shark or sting
ray." *I am babbling.*

"Sounds like fun. Makes me wish I wasn't leaving." He
roughed back his wet hair. "Laura, I'm sorry I blew my
stack again with you. Would you believe you're the only one
I do that to?" he asked, his handsome mouth awry.

"Maybe that's because I'm the only one who keeps
sticking her nose into your business. Would you believe I'm
going to try and stop doing that? Even if it means biting
through my lower lip."

"You leave that lovely lip alone." A hard finger brushed
across the endangered object, then dropped. He glanced at
the boat straining against its tether like a spirited steed. "I'm

glad you're taking John Ed along, I don't like the thought of you venturing out to open sea in a small boat anyway, much less alone.''

Mildly she rebutted, ''I have no problem with it. And I generally do as I please. When are you and Heather leaving?''

''At one. We'd hoped you'd have lunch with us. I'm cooking hamburgers on the grill.''

The strained joviality in his voice made Laura feel better. Deciding not to analyze that, she shook back the braid that tamed her hair. ''Thanks, but they're all waiting,'' she said vaguely. ''Well, you and Heather have a good trip to Raleigh and I . . . guess I'll see you when you get back. 'Bye, Cabe.'' She raised her voice. '''Bye, Heather,'' she called, and walked on.

Eleven

———

Cabe didn't say when he'd be returning and Laura didn't ask, though by Tuesday evening she was wishing she had. "He said he'd be traveling most of the week on business," she replied carelessly when queried on his whereabouts.

Dolly looked at her sharply, but decided not to pry any deeper into the reason for her niece's subdued manner. "I wonder if he'll need a baby-sitter again this weekend? I sure did enjoy watching that little Heather Saturday night. Tucking her in and reading her a bedtime story, makes an old heart young again. Kind of like a parent. Or grandparent."

It was a perfect opening if one overlooked the sly prod she'd stuck in there, Laura thought. Very briefly, she explained Cabe's need for a live-in housekeeper. After her initial pleasure, Dolly's pragmatic nature took over. She couldn't leave the store. Who would look after Pearl?

Pearl had recovered and was vastly indignant that anyone thought she needed looking after. She had always wanted her own private apartment, and besides, it would mean a raise in salary, maybe, eventually, even her own car. Dolly said she'd have to think about it, which aggravated Pearl all the more.

Leaving the two women to their private wrangle, Laura closed out the cash register, picked up the mail and went home before she could be drawn into it.

Except for John Ed, who was painting the wrought-iron fence, Cabe's big house was deserted. She waved, but did not stop. Her own home seemed sterile and empty even with KK's joyous greeting bouncing off its walls. Nibbling on a hot croissant, she sat down at her grandmother's writing desk to sort through the mail.

Dispirited already, her heart sank as she opened an envelope containing the final past-due notice on her property taxes. Included with it was a regretful note from a friend who worked at City Hall. Laura would have to pay in full; they had carried Richards' Country Store as long as legally possible.

Laura's proud carriage slumped. She had to do something, and now, not some comfortably vague tomorrow. But what?

There was always Cabe . . . a hard shake of head instantly rejected that option. Her skin shrank from just the thought of taking money from Cabe.

She had run out of options. Slowly she ran her fingers over the satiny desktop, then opened her wallet and extracted Cord Hunter's business card. Noting his wife's avid interest in the rare antique, he had requested Laura call him should she ever decide to sell it.

The museum-quality heirloom would be displayed to much better effect in the Hunters' luxurious home. Holding that thought in mind, Laura set her mouth and called him.

She arranged to be home, ostensibly for lunch, when a minivan arrived to pick up the desk the following afternoon. She filled its spot with an old churn that held dried grasses. Then she lay down on her bed and wept quietly. After that she washed her face, picked up her books and went to class.

She finished the final exam ahead of schedule and was back at the store by two-thirty. At five, the reporter arrived for Pearl's interview and the day ended on a happier note, at least for the aunts, Laura thought, smiling at their excitement as they bustled about getting things ready. The wispy little newsman roused Dolly's maternal streak. Certain that the poor thing hadn't had a decent meal in years, she invited him to supper.

"I'll make a nice meat loaf," she decided. "Why don't you stay, too, Mary Laura?"

"Thanks, Aunt Dolly, but I think I'll just grab a hot dog in the park, then go on home. I've got things to do tonight," Laura said. Like be alone, she thought as she left the store.

A ball game and the fragrance of hot dogs and fat, warm pretzels had attracted the usual Wednesday evening crowd to the small public park. The festive air drew Laura, too. KK could wait a few more minutes for his dinner, she decided, savoring the minute lift of spirits.

After a few minutes spent watching the ball game she wandered over to where a hotly competitive horseshoe-throwing contest was being kibitzed by a clutch of laughing males. Her sauntering progress through their midst gathered teasing comments that she parried easily and with intriguing lack of interest—until she saw the one who stood leaning indolently against an ancient elm. Laura stopped with a barely suppressed gasp. Cabe was bandying words with the players, but his green eyes were smiling at her.

The unexpected sight of him was an incredible shock of delight. The sun danced in his lustrous dark hair and fired it with highlights. He wore those tight jeans again and a collarless, blue knit shirt.

Apparently he was becoming well known and liked by the locals. The winners were challenging him to a horseshoe

game with a promise of beating his tail off and were razzed
by the audience. Cabe grinned at her and her heart jumped
alarmingly. Those sexy eyes held her to the spot as he ambled to meet her.

He stopped before her and hooked his thumbs in his
pockets. "Hi, pretty lady. Need a ride home?"

"Thanks, but I have a boat."

"Then would you care to break bread with me tonight?"

"I don't know." She glanced at the hot dog cart. "I
haven't decided what I'm going to do for dinner tonight.
Ask me later."

Walking on, Laura smiled to herself as the other males
began riding him about striking out. He hadn't struck out
and in all likelihood, he knew it. But he took his ribbing in
good-natured stride.

She gave the boat full power as soon as she cleared the
marina and arrived home in record time. Her buoyant spirits and cooing baby talk turned KK into an ecstatic, all-over
wriggle. She filled his food and water bowl, then hurried
into the bathroom and ran a bath.

Submerged up to her chin in its steamy bliss, she permitted herself one question. How did she feel about Cabe?
Cautious and a little angry, but eager, too. Joyous, a rare
and special kind of joy. A tiny twinge of panic that stopped
her from probing any deeper. And aroused, she added, relaxing. There was no denying that her entire body was anticipating the next night she would spend with him. Her
stomach quivered as she recalled his potent brand of magic.
Just that green-eyed smile could excite her more than another man's boldest caress.

Hearing KK's warning bark, she got out of the tub and
grabbed a bathsheet. Her heart was a wild thing seeking to
escape its cage. I'm a love-slave, she thought. Amused at her
fancy, she went to the dresser and extracted a bracelet from
her jewelry box. She clamped the wide gold band around her
upper arm. Studying its effect, she threw back her head and
laughed in a way that would have curled a man's toes.

Cabe rapped on the door. A provocative, purely feminine glint lit her eyes. "It's open, Cabe," she called. "I'm in the bedroom. Come sit and talk to me while I finish dressing." Beguilingly innocent, she smiled as he made his way to the open bedroom door. Her pulse was going crazy. "I won't be long, believe me," she assured him. "I'm starving!"

The corners of his mouth turned up wickedly. "I'm hungry, too, Laura," Cabe murmured, letting his deliberate gaze flow over her from tousled head to bare toes. The pink bathsheet clung to her breasts in breathtaking defiance of gravity, highlighting every damp valley and gentle slope in its graceful fall to the floor. The lines of her neck and shoulder were astonishingly fragile and beautiful, while the bracelet on her naked arm gave her the look of a woman chained by the power of a man's passion. Fueled by the most primitive male needs, the flame of Cabe's masculinity burned hot and bright. He would have fought another male barehanded for the right to claim and mate with this seductive female. "Very hungry," he repeated.

The gold sparks glinting in his emerald eyes left no doubt of his meaning. Pretending ignorance, neither inviting nor rejecting, Laura assured him they'd dine shortly. She lifted her arms to unpin her hair. When she tipped back her head to brush it, the gold-washed mane reached to the small of her back.

Cabe crossed to her. "May I?" Taking the brush, he began drawing it through the silky mass while she stood mesmerized.

Her melting response to the tender, possessive gesture stripped Laura of defenses and evoked a feathery sense of fear. She raised her chin for a direct look into his heavy-lidded eyes.

"What were you doing in the park, Cabe?"

"Looking for you. Your aunts said you'd be there and I had to see you as soon as possible. I won't say why, but it had to do with keeping my sanity."

Laura ignored his drawling tone and cut right to the heart of his remark. "You missed me? Oh Cabe, I missed you, too. So much. I thought of you constantly—did you think of me?"

"Now and then a stray thought of you did occur to me."

"Don't tease."

"Okay. Only when I wasn't sleeping." His voice vibrated against her smooth back. He gathered up her hair and swept it aside to bare her tender nape. His warm lips touched there. "That's why I came back today." Bending his head lower, he branded her shoulders with tiny, hot kisses. "It wasn't practical, I'll have to return Saturday morning. But every time I thought of you, I forgot practicality."

He tossed the brush in the general direction of the counter. "I forgot everything but the need to be with you...." His hands encircled her towel-wrapped hips. "To make love to you." They pressed her backward and fit her compliant curves to rock-hard muscles. "To hold you all through the night, wake up with you in my arms..." His palms slid around the front of her hips and bridged the soft flesh in between. "And make love to you again," he ended in a passion-slurred whisper.

Her eyes locked with his in the mirror. Wherever their bodies touched, the heat of friction sent excitement spinning out along exquisitely sensitive curves and muscled flesh alike. Moaning softly, she turned in his hands and murmured something, but he couldn't make out what. His pounding heartbeat filled his ears with the tumultuous sound of white-water rapids.

She plucked at his shirttail. With a lithe twist of body, he pulled the shirt over his head, after which he peeled the towel from her.

The potent stimulation of soft hands slipping beneath the waistband of his jeans provoked a groan she muffled with her bewitching mouth. "Why is it," she asked between kisses, "that you can undress me with a flick of fingers, but I must work all manner of zippers and buttons on you?"

He laughed, low and rough. Her breasts pressed into his chest inflamingly. Her nipples were already tight and erect. He cupped them and felt the puckered tips become satiny beads beneath his massaging thumbs. He bit her ear. "Only one zipper. Undo it."

Beautifully compliant, Laura unzipped his jeans and slid them down his taut hips to his feet. Her hair brushed against his charged flesh as she slowly knelt to slip off his shoes. He wore nothing else, a fact she noted with a smoky laugh. She felt just as he did. It was in her glowing dark eyes, in the allurement of her curving mouth.

She kissed his knees and an astonished quill of excitement streaked through him from that point upward. Rising, she allowed her palm to brush over the thrillingly tangible evidence of his desire. He sucked in his breath. Control fled. He spread a hand across her bottom and crooked the other around the back of her neck, securing for himself a captive maiden. His head lowered and his mouth came crashing down. She grasped handfuls of his hair and opened her lips to the hungry invasion of his tongue. A dozen heartbeats later he pushed her down on the bed and lowered himself over her. Her feathery caresses roamed down his tensing back, rippling his hot skin with tiny shudders. She wanted more of his mouth, and took it. Words escaped from his mind with each ragged breath. "Darlin', little darlin'," he whispered thickly into her sweet mouth.

Together they rode ecstasy's wild flight to the stars. Together they shared the lovely, languid free-fall back to a world made more splendid by that profoundly simple word.

Cabe broke the euphoric hush with an accusing mumble. "I'm hungry."

Laura sighed. "Me, too." She stretched, luxuriously. "You called me darling. Several times you did."

Cabe's mouth quirked. "I've called you lots of things in the past two months. I just haven't said them aloud."

"Why did you stop fighting it, Cabe? Us, I mean."

It was a question Cabe had asked himself. "I suppose because a man can only fight himself for so long. Resisting you isn't the easiest thing I've ever done. I guess also because I finally began seeing you as a strong, mature woman instead of the soft, crushable illusion I started out with." He tipped her face to his, his eyes intense. "There's no slowing this now, babe, no going back. It's like wildfire, unstoppable."

"Babe. I like that," she decided. The remark, though true, was merely a delaying tactic. She was remembering his disproportionate bitterness and hostility toward his ex-wife. Questions arose; she thrust them back down. But this sudden sharp infusion of doubt made her keenly aware of how fragile a claim she had on him. "No, no going back." She touched her fingertips to kiss-swollen lips, then to his firm mouth. With a bravery she had to work at, she said, "Here's to the future and what it holds for us."

"Food, I hope." He caught her fingers and nibbled on them. With a saucy laugh she leaned over him and whispered something deliciously erotic. Then she rolled onto her back and pulled him down to her. "Laura, I'm totally depleted," he warned.

Her mouth pressed against his throat to nip and lick while her nails raked down his back to his powerful buttocks. "No, you're not," she said.

"No, I'm not," he said...

The sound of ragged breaths slowly calmed to murmurous silence. This time it was Laura who surfaced first from the golden haze of fulfillment. "Cabe?"

"Um?"

"If I lie in this position much longer, I'm going to resemble a pancake."

"Lord, we don't want that!" Pushing himself up and off of her, he flopped onto his back. "Food, woman!"

"Good idea. But I don't feel like getting dressed.... I know, we'll raid the refrigerator."

Cabe opened one eye. "With what you keep in there?"

"Humph. You still like peanut butter?" she asked after a moment of thought. He did. Stepping over his shirt, she donned a thigh-length wrapper and went to the kitchen.

Pulling on his jeans, Cabe wandered barefoot to the sink where she was slicing two French mini-loaves in halves lengthwise. As bidden, he carried two glasses and a pitcher of icy milk to the table. Passing their plates, Laura grabbed cloth napkins and sat down opposite him.

He bit into the crusty sandwich. "Hey, this is delicious—what all's on here?"

"Just peanut butter topped with sweetened and sliced fresh strawberries. Messy, but good." Thinking rapidly, she delicately touched the napkin to her lips. Cabe so seldom asked about her private life, past or future, that she still felt uneasy prying into his. But to her way of thinking, physical intimacy went hand in hand with verbal intimacy. "Cabe, how do you feel about Michele?"

The milk Cabe was lifting to his lips halted in mid-air. He gave a short laugh—how often had he wondered the very same thing? "Let's just say there's no love lost between us."

"But there *is* love lost between you," she reminded softly.

"Was." He drained his glass and poured another.

"All right, was," she agreed, not knowing quite what she was agreeing to, but knowing intuitively that it was wise to do so. "Are you two...civilized with each other?"

"Of course. She is the mother of my child."

Laura heard the faint edge in his voice. But she was incapable of halfway concerns. "Then you're going to honor her request to take Heather? She does have that right, Cabe."

"No," he said quietly. "Any rights she had were rendered null and void the day she left us."

Wanting with all her heart to erase the shadows flickering at the back of his eyes, Laura leaned forward, her voice persuasively earnest. "I know that was a terrible experience for you, but don't hate her for it. Instead you should pity her, Cabe. It's you Heather loves and trusts, you're the one she idolizes. All Michele has are memories and guilt.''

"I doubt she has any guilt, but that's beside the point. Look, I know you're only trying to help," he said patiently. "but in this instance you can't. Heather's my responsibility, which is scary as hell, but it's up to me to decide what's best for her. And I don't think being pulled this way and that just to gratify a selfish woman's whim is it.''

"No, of course not, but I don't think that'll be the case. Heather's curious about her mother, Cabe, and it's perfectly natural to want to satisfy that curiosity.''

He didn't reply. Studying his sharply defined profile, loving its austere purity, Laura sighed and spread her hands, palms out, mollifyingly. "I know it's your decision, but I— I just had to have my say. And now that I have, I won't bring it up again. Want another sandwich?''

He thought he could eat another. She stood up and turned toward the sink. The silky wrapper caught on the high slopes of her buttocks, revealing, as she walked, two enchanting little half moons of curvy flesh. Cabe's breath hung up, then flowed through his closed lips unsteadily. The feeling that came over him was indescribable. It contained a healthy amount of masculine lust, but the rest was of the heart, tremendous, impossible to label, both weakening and strengthening at the same time.

The urge to lower all safeguards and let everything spill out, his anger, his bitterness and hurts, his tenderest, most secretive feelings, was a gnawing ache in his heart.

But he couldn't, not yet. He was a thinking man with a thinking man's principles and too much was happening to him too fast. Better to analyze his feelings than to give in to impulses that he—or even worse, she—would later regret.

Over her shoulder she smiled at him. But her stubborn chin and the way she held it betrayed the resilience and grit in her. Confusion crept into his heart. He had always done the nurturing, had always been the one to hold and soothe and protect. But he needed to feel her arms around him, holding him with that tensile strength, keeping him safe, and he wasn't sure men ought to feel like that.

"Laura, please, come here," said Cabe softly. Wrapping his arms around her, he drew her between his knees. "I do want to spend the night with you, very much. But John Ed'll be on the job early in the morning and I doubt that we'll be able to keep others from knowing about our—" he hesitated "—intimate relationship. I know you're a proud woman and that that would hurt you, and I simply cannot stand the thought of you getting hurt, in any way—"

A regal lift of hand cut him off. "You're right, I am a proud woman. And one of the things I'm proudest of is us. If I'm supposed to feel shame that you chose me to satisfy your needs, then I'm in trouble, because I'd proclaim it from the top of city hall if it was up to me."

Her lips moved wryly. "But I'm sure some people would feel awkward about that, including yourself. So early tomorrow morning you'll presumably come over to invite me for a walk along the river, which is a lovely thing to do, so we will. As for being hurt..." She drew his head against her breasts, her voice husky with the fear that still nibbled at her confidence. "I'm not afraid of risk, Cabe. I love you—"

Laura stilled, struggling for the air that shock had just expelled from her lungs. Her affection for him had flowed into love so quietly that she felt stunned at the realization.

She sensed his tension, heard it in his strained voice as he said her name. Shushing him, she unlocked her painfully tight clasp of fingers and continued lightly, "I'm not telling you this because I expect reciprocative words from you—I don't expect anything from you, Cabe. I think what we have is wonderful and I hope that something even more wonderful will come out of it, but if it doesn't, well, that won't alter the fact that it was a many splendored thing."

The pulsing hollow of her throat felt the warm press of his mouth. "My precious Mary Laura. You humble me, you know," he said so softly she had to bend her head to hear it.

Laura clutched his shoulders; being deemed precious had a dissolving affect on her bones. It didn't mean he loved her. But it came very close.

"Good morning, sleepyhead! Coffee's on, breakfast will be ready in twenty minutes. Scrambled eggs okay?"

"Scrambled is fine." Laura experienced a delicious shock of delight as she responded to the man who stood on her bedroom balcony watching the billowing gold and pink clouds of a breezy sunrise. Although nearly two weeks had passed, this was only their sixth time to share morning's first light together. With Heather and Dolly living in his house, Cabe spent the night only when his need to hold and be held overcame caution. But waking up to him felt so right and natural that it was as if all her days had started like this.

She no longer felt afraid of loving him. Why should I be? she thought with a defiant toss of her head. What they meant to each other was clearly expressed in every tender word, look and touch.

His quick smile stirred the dregs of morning desire like snow in a paperweight. His hair, merrily tousled by the wind, was shot through with coppery glints. The dark green eyes glowed with the vibrant life and sexuality that were so inseparably entwined. Rolled-up sleeves and an open collar showed smooth, taut skin; a gray-and-white striped shirt and darker gray slacks stressed the long lines of his body.

Laura felt a gust of pride as she looked at him, the pride of knowing that, for the moment, she owned that magnificent body. It was oddly untainted by hope or regret. She simply wanted to shout it to the world that this man came to her at night and to no other.

"Shower or eat first?" he asked.

"Shower first, I think." Laura raked her hands through the sleep-tangled mane drifting around her shoulders. She looked rather like an untamed tigress. Which is not a bad way to look when you have a tiger on your balcony, she thought whimsically, and threw him a kiss through the open door. With that light, almost weightless posture, he really did remind her of a sleek cat. Flinging back the quilt, she reached for her shorty, ruffly pink wrapper. "What did you do, go walking without me?"

"Just a short one. You were sleeping so good." As she tied the sash around her waist, Cabe closed the door behind him and drew the draperies again. Capturing her moving figure, he inhaled her sweet, musky scent with intense male pleasure. "You know what you look like in that thing?" he asked, cuddling her closer. "A cute little sexpot."

Laura didn't mind being a cute little sexpot, quite the contrary. She reveled in the names he called her. She reveled in him. His hands had gotten loose under the wrapper. "Breakfast?" she reminded. "I do have to work today."

After a kiss that reestablished who was in charge here, Cabe let her go. He felt nervous about such an enormity of emotion, but like her declaration of love, the radiant warmth it created was impossible to deal with rationally.

He opened the bedroom door and KK romped in with the ear-splitting noise by which schnauzers express their feelings. Cabe went on to the kitchen. As usual, passing the spot where Laura's writing desk had stood tightened his jaw. But he hadn't mentioned its disappearance.

Breakfast was on the table when she waltzed into the kitchen. With KK lying at her feet, they talked as they ate, a domestic interlude that Cabe enjoyed too much for his peace of mind. Not having this rare pleasure was becoming more and more unthinkable.

"Sure you don't want me to drive you to work?" he asked before leaving. The day had become overcast. She shook her head; she'd take the boat. "Stubbornnest chin in the world. Okay. See you tonight, doll."

Laura laughed delightedly. No other man she knew had the nerve to call a contemporary woman such a warm, funny, breezy endearment. Some, less secure in themselves, would have thought it demeaning. She accepted it for the lovely verbal hug it was.

Snapping his fingers for the dog, Cabe walked on to his own house. Heather came running out. Her face glowed. She's happy, he thought, his heart swelling again. She greeted both him and KK with moist, nuzzling kisses. "I'm glad I got mine first," he told Dolly. "Oh, don't bother with breakfast for me—I had a bite with Laura." He glanced at his watch. "Well, I've got to run. I'll have dinner at home tonight," the master of the house said masterfully.

He stopped off at his first-floor office to make a few telephone calls. One was to Cord Hunter, who was in Raleigh for the weekend.

"Have you made a decision yet?"

"Cabe," his friend sighed. "This really that important to you?"

"Let me put it this way. How would you feel if circumstances forced Juliet to sell a precious family heirloom?"

A note of humorous curiosity entered Cord's voice. "Isn't there a slight difference in the two situations?"

Cabe chuckled. "Maybe a little. But the hurt's the same. And you know how fond I am of Laura."

"Personally I think you're a little more than just fond, but that's beside the point. Juliet sure does love that desk, Cabe. It's already situated in a place of honor in our California home. But all right, let me talk to her about it."

"I'll be calling back tomorrow, so talk well." Frowning, Cabe replaced the receiver. He disliked pressuring a friend. But the sight of Laura's pretty face lighting up as he came into the store half an hour later stiffened his resolve.

Pearl greeted him happily. Her newspaper interview had been a whopping success. Not only did it give her a heady little taste of fame, but it led to the sale of several pictures, among them two large, more costly works. Looking ever so smart and stylish in her spiffy new wheaten suit and lavender-blue blouse, she stood with a "client" in the storeroom, which now housed a miniature art gallery down one side of the wall. A comfortably wide aisle had been cleared and carpeted, and inexpensive floodlights mounted. Her imagination did the rest.

"She's so happy, Cabe. Thank you," Laura said very softly. "Now stop that—I know you arranged that interview, so don't act as if you haven't the faintest idea what I mean!"

Cabe looked as if he hadn't the faintest idea what she meant.

He was feeling frisky. While she snapped the lid on his container of coffee, he leaned close to say out of the corner of his mouth, "I'll see you tonight, babe—just as soon as I can make a clean getaway!"

Laughter erupted, the kind that wells up free of restraint and is full of shared secrets. Deciding he'd better leave before Pearl and her customer had something else to speculate about, he took his coffee to the car. What was happening to him? he wondered as he wheeled away from the curb. Why did he walk around feeling so unbelievably, extraordinarily high? What had she done to him?

The answer came that evening shortly after dinner when the telephone rang. His caller was Michele. She was in Raleigh, and would like to see him. To talk about Heather, she admitted, her fluting voice lowering to a small chuckle, but also to see him. It had been a while.

To his mild astonishment, Cabe spoke calmly and without the gritty constriction of throat he had come to associate with Michele. He still said no, but the biting sarcasm was missing.

It was only later, when he finally filled his needful arms with Laura, that he could put words to the vast change she had made in him. She had cleansed him of his cynical distrust, and given him the courage to hope again. Under the influence of her goodness and loving warmth, the corrosive bitterness and anger created by Michele's desertion had been greatly diminished. She had even prodded him into that, he thought, smiling into her exquisite face.

Laura stretched up to kiss him for long, lovely moments. Then she took his hand and led him to the bedroom. "Sit, please," she said. "Tonight it's your turn to be loved and cherished."

He smiled, liking how easily she used those two beautiful words. Obedient, he dropped onto the bed, his expression bemused as she said, "I splurged on this just for you," and pulled her flowered shift over her head to reveal a tailored, champagne-colored satin teddy cut high on the elegant legs finished off with backless, high-heeled satin slippers.

"Whatever the price," he said with raw huskiness, "it was worth it."

"Thank you. Uh-uh, do not touch, please," she said sternly. Again he obeyed, his eyes hooding as she knelt to remove his shoes and socks. Her soft hands slid over his feet and up to his thighs, a teasing massage that sent running fire through his entire lower torso. Standing over him, she began unbuttoning his shirt while he sat very still and clenched his aching hands. Disobedient, they traced the line of satin up as far as it went, and down even farther before she halted his explorations. "Lie back, please," she instructed with that delicious primness so at odds with her sultry eyes and saucy, tip-tongued smile.

After stealing a kiss, he complied. "Have I told you that you're one of the sexiest men I've ever met?" she asked.

"The first day we met, if memory serves me right," he replied in a voice reminiscent of roughened velvet. "I wanted to throw you down and make love to you right there on the terrace."

Her gaze drifted languidly to his. "I doubt I'd have stopped you." Undoing his trousers, she drew them down his long legs. Then she let her hands map the planes and contours of his body, inch by slow, maddening, skyrocketing inch.

When she had reduced him to a column of flame, she stood up and worked the satin straps off her shoulders, one at a time; with beguiling grace she slipped the garment down her flawless body. She straddled his thighs and crouched over him tantalizingly, her hair veiling her face and various parts of his upper torso as she scattered kisses here and there. When he could stand it no more, Cabe pulled her down atop him and asserted his mastery in the age-old way of a man with a maid.

It was quiet, euphoric lovemaking. They felt no frenzied urge to end it, no need for fast, rough movements. Just lying together, sharing the rapturous sensation of filling and of being filled, of sensuously slow, deep kisses taken and given, was profoundly pleasing. She rose up on her arms and pleasured his mouth and chest with her jewel-tipped breasts. With his lips he traced the shape of her face and delighted in knowing the delicate lines of her features by taste alone.

"This is wonderful," he said. Her response was a kiss so sweet he felt as if he was drowning in the honeyed cave of her mouth. He tasted it again and again while the rich, hot spiral of excitement coiled higher and higher. Ecstasy's explosion flung them from the world, a flight into a hot, bright sky that left them utterly drained, and blissfully fulfilled.

Cabe lay holding her with a kind of awed wonder. After all the lonely months of feelings that were about as profound as the ripples from a stone tossed into a pond, to feel so much so deeply so intensely was a sublime experience. His defensive walls, already badly eroded, were crumbling with each breath he drew. He wanted to open up to her, hold nothing back. But the subject that needed talking about was embarrassingly intimate, and he was a shy man for all his worldly airs.

He had never discussed his vasectomy with a woman. It wasn't something a man just tossed into the conversation, he thought, dry-humored. He closed his eyes and sought a way to begin.

Stirring from her half-drowse, Laura nestled closer to his big, warm body. It's just like my dream, she thought. All that's missing is a baby fussing somewhere. She laughed throatily as another thought occurred to her.

"What?" Cabe asked lovingly.

"I'm not sure I ought to say. You might not like it."

"What? Tell me."

"Okay. I was thinking about the baby you and I could make and what a threat we'd unleash upon the world. With my good looks and your sexy green eyes—Lord, but he'd be a ladykiller!"

Cabe knew she heard the breath he expelled. "It is nice, imagining you with my baby." Smiling at her soft gasp, he turned onto his back and drew her head to his shoulders. "But that's all it is, imagination, all it will ever be." He drew another deep breath. "Laura, right after our twins were born, I had a vasectomy. I couldn't give you a baby even if you did want it."

Twelve

—

Laura jerked up with a strangled sound that fell between a laugh and a cry. She stared at him, seeking humor, however incomprehensible it was. Seeing none, she shook her head in fierce denial. "No! Cabe, say you don't mean that!"

Cabe exhaled unsteadily. Her reaction had hit him like a stiff-fingered blow to the solar plexus.

"I can't, Laura."

"You can't?" Her expression of stunned disbelief flowed from forced acceptance into outrage. "You mean you really did... Oh, Cabe, how could you? I love you! I wanted to have your children—I want it so bad I hurt!" Before Cabe could absorb the shock of her outcry, the sudden fury that distorted her pretty face imprinted itself on his cheek in the shape of five slender fingers.

Her hands flew to her mouth. Horrified, she stared at the reddening marks, her eyes huge. She had stunned herself. "Oh, Cabe, I'm sorry." Her face crumpled. "Why? Why did you?"

Cabe fixed his gaze on the ceiling. "Michele nearly died giving birth. We couldn't afford the risk of it happening again."

His voice was dispassionate. Hers was acrid and angry. "So you made the noble sacrifice. And she let you."

"She didn't 'let' me do anything. It was entirely my decision."

"And then she left you."

"Yes."

A smothery silence fell between them. With noticeable lack of grace, she moved to the edge of the bed and sat with her shoulders hunched. "I just do not understand how you could bring yourself to do something like that, I just do not."

"Laura—" Supporting himself on an elbow, Cabe put a hand on her back.

She flinched. "Don't."

He released her, his mouth compressing to a hard line as the pain of her rejection slammed into him. Rolling out of bed, he thrust his legs into his trousers and fastened them with trembling fingers. Anger flared, blinding white behind his eyelids.

"It was necessary, okay? And I don't consider what I did stupid, either. It was an honorable solution to a serious problem."

"I suppose it was," she replied dully. "Why didn't you tell me about it sooner?"

"Would it have made any difference?"

"I don't know. But you should have told me."

"Laura, I didn't say anything because—well, it's just not something a man brings up without good reason." Aching for the words he wasn't hearing, he sat down beside her and roughed up his hair. "I didn't think it was important—I had no intention of getting involved with you. And when I realized I had no choice in the matter, I shoved it aside—told myself it was no big deal. But you're right, I should have told you."

She didn't reply. Unable to withstand her remoteness, he said cautiously, "Laura, vasectomies can be reversed—"

Her brilliant dark eyes glanced off his face. "Cabe, I keep up-to-date on things, I know the enormous odds against that, even with today's modern technology. And the odds expand with time."

Momentarily silenced, he searched through the incredible mess she had made of his mind. He wanted to rebut, but he had no ammunition. He had been advised prior to carrying through his decision that the degree of reversibility was very limited, and to regard it as permanent.

"You called our friendship a many splendored thing, and I agree, it's that and more," he said, very low. Invitingly, he paused. Silence. Unable to dredge up the cynicism he so desperately needed, his next words emerged as a stark plea. "Surely my ability—or inability—to reproduce doesn't change that?"

"Cabe, please, I . . ." Shaking her head, she helplessly spread her hands. "I have some thinking to do."

His voice was bitter. "Yeah. Looks like I do, too." Hurting more than he thought possible, Cabe slipped on his shoes, grabbed up his shirt and walked out the door.

Laura didn't try to stop him. She felt shell-shocked. Nothing functioned right, not even her thinking processes. The prospect of having to choose between having the man she loved and the babies her powerful maternal drive demanded had thrown her into a turmoil of painful confusion. She sat impossibly stiff until the front door closed. Then she collapsed on the bed like a rag doll.

Cabe tramped through the black night with little regard to where his feet led him. He felt too raw and battered to reason anything out, and too badly shaken to sleep. He damned her as he stumbled along the riverbank path he had so lightheartedly walked this morning. He hurled at her the blame for his bleak misery. But his implacable sense of self-honesty soon refused to accept that. He had only himself to blame. He had wanted to believe that children of her own weren't all that important to Laura. So he did.

Some foolish, ungovernable part of his mind had begun whispering of a second chance at happiness and he had held onto his seductive delusion. And when your pretty bubble bursts, he derided himself savagely, you want to cry like some mistreated kid.

The raging heat inside him abruptly died, leaving a hollow iciness where it had been. He shivered, chilled inside despite the balmy temperature. "Damn her," he whispered, then caught himself up sharply. The metallic taste of bitter hurt and anger that etched his mouth was all too familiar. He wasn't going to get trapped in that dark ugliness again. Wearily he turned his feet toward home and bed.

He fell asleep with Laura on his mind and awoke to her vivid image. The hurt was still with him, and would be for a long, long time, he suspected. But he was thinking clearly again. And what he was thinking was wretchedly logical. He would simply have to forget Laura.

He was a strong man, Cabe reminded himself as jagged shards of pain pushed through his icy shield. He could do it. With a little more effort he could go back to the way it had been before he bought this house.

He hadn't needed anyone then. He didn't need anyone now.

Stooping, he picked up Heather's kitten and caressed the silky fur. The harsh lines of his face softened as a positive thought emerged. At least one good thing had come out of all this emotional and mental activity, the objectivity to screen out personal resentments and focus on what was best for his daughter.

It wasn't easy. Even though his darker feelings toward Michele had pretty much dissipated, there was still a sore spot. Perhaps there always would be, Cabe reflected. He was only human. But another thing Laura had done for him was start him thinking with a father's viewpoint instead of a vengeful man's. He glanced at his watch. Nearly seven;

surely Michele was up by now. Hearing Dolly and Heather's sleepy voices, he went back to his bedroom and dialed his ex-wife's number.

Across the way, Laura sat on the edge of her bed holding KK and torturing herself. The events of last night rolled through her mind starkly. A dull sense of shame surfaced from her unstable mix of emotions. She had behaved badly last night.

"But it was the shock!" she whispered beseeching. It had washed through her like scalding water.

Striking him—she flinched at memory of that atrocity—had been a gut-instinct reaction to a devastating blow. Still she couldn't defend her behavior. Withdrawing into herself was none too admirable, either, but how else could she have borne the searing wave of disappointment that still swept through her each time dreams and reality collided? Confusingly, she thought of Cabe and how much he had been hurt, and she hated someone. Herself, maybe.

Realizing she wasn't getting anywhere, Laura dressed in jogging attire and set out for the river path. Heather was in the yard romping with her kitten. She waved. Laura waved back. Remembering Cabe's stunning revelation last night, a hollow reed of ache started up. How he must have resented my know-it-all lecture on raising his child, she thought disgustedly. There was no sign of him. Had there been, she might have gone to him. But the terrace remained devoid of life.

The day dragged on interminably. Around three o'clock she picked up KK and headed for the pier. Maybe a boat ride would give her the perspective she needed.

As they cut across the rear of Cabe's yard, the dog's excited barking attracted Heather's attention. "Laura! Hi! Where are you going? Can I go, too?" she asked, running to meet them. She wore a yellow sunsuit and she looked like a sunbeam, Laura thought.

"No, honey, I'm going out on the boat." Laura glanced at the house. "What's your daddy up to today?" she asked brightly.

"He's gone somewhere. Why can't I go with you? I'll be good," the little girl assured her.

"But you're..." Laura paused, shaken by her sudden realization. Bending, she clasped the child's shoulders and asked softly, "You aren't afraid to ride in the boat anymore?"

Heather hesitated and licked her lips. "Maybe just a little bit. But you'll be there. And KK isn't afraid. So I won't be, either," she decided stoutly.

"Well, okay, then," Laura said, relieved. "Let's go ask Aunt Dolly!"

A few minutes later, with permission granted on the promise to return within the hour, Laura put her crew aboard and set a course for the jewellike islets that so intrigued Heather. Up close, they appeared to be mostly marsh, inhabited by a variety of scurrying, hopping, crawling wildlife that, though undoubtedly fascinating, nonetheless kept the two observers inside the boat.

"Fantastic!" Heather declared, her current favorite applicable-to-everything word.

Laura took a great breath of invigorating sea air. "Fantastic!" she agreed. Oh, Cabe, her heart cried, if you could see this! Her eyes clouded. Swiftly she blocked the other thoughts constricting her chest. Nothing was going to ruin this pleasant interlude.

Leaving the maze behind them, they headed for another, larger isle that boasted a crescent of white sand beach. They were nearly there when the motor sputtered and died.

"Out of gas—but no problem," she assured Heather. "We'll just hook up the auxiliary tank." Making her way to the rear of the gently rocking boat, Laura knelt beside the two big red containers and switched the fuel hose from one to the other.

The engine fired, but refused to catch. Baffled, she looked around, searching for other boats. There were none. They were out of the heavily traveled water lanes. Hiding her twinge of anxiety from watchful green eyes, she went to the stern to re-check the fuel hose.

No problem there. Unthinkingly she lifted the auxiliary tank—and froze in disbelief as it came up easily in her hand. Both tanks were empty!

Laura rocked back on her heels. It couldn't be. Her one cardinal rule was *never* to leave shore without a spare tank of gas. It had been full when she anchored last night, she had checked. Who had used the boat this morning? Probably the teenager down the street. He borrowed it sometimes to run his crab traps— The question of blame flew from mind as Laura grasped the seriousness of her predicament. She was sitting here with a child, a dog, a disabled boat and no immediate means of rectifying the situation.

The key word was immediate. The Cape Fear River ran swift and deep. Its strong current could sweep a boat out to open sea within a very short time. If anything happened to Heather— Now stop that! Laura admonished herself. Nothing's going to happen to Heather or to KK—not if you stop squatting here like a paralytic frog and *do* something!

Galvanized to action, she scrambled around the seat and searched under the forward hold for her emergency oar. "Found it!" she cried triumphantly. Bracing herself against the boat's motion, she located the isle they had meant to visit. If they could reach it, they'd be safe.

That was a fairly big if, but they were drifting too rapidly to waste time worrying. Thrusting the oar into the water, she began stroking, first from one side and then the other, expertly. She glanced at Heather. The emerald eyes were enormous in her tiny face. Stricken, Laura forced a look of comical exasperation.

"Both tanks empty. Darn! Wouldn't you know that the very first time I get to take you out in my boat, something...like this would happen?" she grumbled, grunting with exertion in between sentences. "But there's nothing to worry about, it's going to be all right, I'm going to row us...over there to that little isle. See it? You just sit there and hold KK for me, okay? Sometimes that dog..." she chattered on gaily, inanely, "sometimes he thinks if we're going slow enough, why, he can just jump out and walk on the water."

Heather's weak giggle was encouraging. Laura talked until her throat hurt and her breath came in soft pants from her endeavors. Was the isle any closer? Half the time the endlessly rolling waves obscured her vision until she couldn't tell if they were making any headway or not.

As the roar of the surf grew louder, Heather's face grew even whiter, if possible. The mixed currents swirling around the snaggle-toothed rocks that guarded the entrance to the beach were tossing them about like a hapless wood chip.

The shining crescent of sand seemed to mock her as Laura fought the breaking surf, trying to set a course that would keep her clear of those ominous black rocks. She wasn't at all sure she could maneuver that well with one oar. Remembering how she used to body surf, she wondered if the same principle would work on a small boat. It was worth a try, she thought, gritting her teeth as the boat angled sideways in spite of her efforts.

When the needed wave appeared on the horizon, she began paddling frantically to turn the bow shoreward. There wasn't enough time, the great swell had already started. With a thunderous roar, the huge wave crested under the boat, picked it up terrifyingly—and shot it past the rocks to the beach.

They landed sideways, upright. The rush of adrenaline carried Laura up and out of the boat before she had formed a conscious thought. She deposited her two charges on the sand, tore off her wet life jacket, then splashed back through the shallow water to lift the motor and set the anchor.

When she returned to shore, Heather was standing in the same spot. Her eyes never left Laura's face as she took off the much smaller jacket. "I wasn't a-scared," she declared, blinking furiously at tears.

"Oh, darling, it's all right to be scared. I was." Heather was trembling. Dropping to her knees, Laura drew the child close and held her with a gentle rocking movement.

Two fragile arms wound desperately tight around Laura's neck. Her eyes burned as she cradled the sturdy little body in a fiercely protective embrace. It was a shock to realize how much she loved this small creature, so vulnerable, so dependent, so heart-shakingly precious.

Shivering inside, hardly daring to breathe, Laura expanded her realization, at first cautiously, then with exultance. Her desire to cuddle her own firstborn child like this was still as strong as ever and probably always would be, she acknowledged with soft, intense wistfulness. But her love for Cabe and his daughter was far, far stronger.

Why hadn't she known last night? Laura demanded of herself joyously. No matter, she knew it now. A life without Cabe was unthinkable.

Heather drew back and raised her head. "I'll go look for shells now...." She hesitated, her eyes suddenly fearful again. "But how are we going to get them home to Daddy, Laura?"

A gleeful laugh scratched its way through Laura's throat. "Now don't you know your daddy will be roaring around ordering boats to get out here and get us the second he realizes we're late? You know how he is about people being late! Now you and KK go play and have fun. Did you know you can chase sandpipers forever and never catch one?"

As they ran off to test her claim, Laura collapsed on the sand. A shudder walked down her spine, vertebra by vertebra, in an enormous release of tension. Tears of sheer relief streamed down her face. When they had run their course she got the two flares she carried and sat down to wait for a passing boat.

Exactly one hour and twenty minutes later, she fired the first flare. It was wet, a dud. The second, however, soared into the sky in a burst of orange-gold. Within a wonderfully short time, the handsome sloop she had spied in the distance was making its careful way to the beach.

Quickly Laura explained the situation. When the gas she requested had been transferred to her fuel tank, she asked the sloop's captain to follow her home, for Heather's peace of mind more than anything else. He also agreed to radio the Coast Guard and ask them to notify Cabe that they'd been found.

"I liked it there," Heather said as they left the small isle. "Can we come back someday with Daddy?"

"You bet we can!" Laura replied. She glanced at the white-knuckled grip Heather kept on the handrail. "You okay, sweetheart?"

The golden head bobbed up and down. "We had us quite an adventure today, didn't we!" Laura persisted, watching the heart-shaped face alertly. "And we were both so brave!"

"Oh, yes!" Heather laughed. "Just wait till we tell Daddy!"

Laura's smile vanished. Yes, she thought, just wait. We've been gone three hours now. Everyone must be worried to death about us. Especially Cabe. But it'll be all right, she soothed herself. Oh, he'll have to blow off some steam first. But then...her chin tilted up as she thought of what she had to tell him. She knew exactly how he'd react, with joy and love and then a fierce, virile display of that love.

The nerves in her stomach fluttered anticipatingly. Of course he had never actually told her he loved her, not in words. But she knew—she didn't need words. She was frighteningly happy.

There was a small mob waiting at the foot of Cabe's back yard: Dolly and Pearl, John Ed, Cabe and a woman. The latter two people hurried to the pier as Laura placed the boat alongside with pleasing precision. In the instant between turning off the key and turning to face them, she recognized the beautiful female with a jolt not unlike a sharp slap in the face. Michele!

Rendered confused and uncertain by this astonishing turn of events, Laura pushed up her sunglasses and looked at Cabe.

The dark green eyes blazing into hers were twin thunderstorms. "Are you all right?" he rapped out, swinging toward her. She simply nodded.

"Daddy, Daddy!" Heather cried, and scrambled across the boat into his reaching hands. Michele stepped up beside him and flung her arms around them both, creating a beautiful family circle.

Watching them together, Laura felt a savage stab of pain. Her vision blurred. She stepped onto the pier, her lips stretched in what she hoped was a smile. Behind her the sloop's horn tooted a farewell. She responded with a robotic wave. Her aunts still waited at a distance, she noted distractedly. Apparently they were giving Cabe time for a private reunion. Blanking her mind until she could handle the chilling suspicions growing there, she pulled down her sunglasses and waited, too.

Chaotic seconds passed before Cabe could function properly and so he did nothing to shatter the illusion of togetherness. Incredibly, his powerful legs were rubbery. After an eon of agonizing uncertainty, the relief of their safe return was honey and wine pouring through hollow bones. And then came the wild anger! His dark head lifted as it flooded his system and escaped in a blast of loving fury, similar to that of parents whose carelessly straying child has been restored to them and it's impossible to decide whether to hug or strangle.

He looked at the woman who had been responsible for two of the most torturous hours of his life, wondering if his only reasons for living were, even now—even as he paced the den, paced the terrace, paced the pier—lying beneath the Cape Fear's deep, dark waters.

The rage was murderous, wonderful, uncontaminated by reason. "What the blue-blazing *hell*," he exploded, "did you think you were doing going clear out to Pelican's Isle with my daughter in that—that fiberglass cigar! What on earth possessed you to place yourselves in such peril?"

Laura paled. "Cabe, I've gone out there dozens of times without incident. You know I wouldn't endanger Heather—"

"She *was* endangered, and so were you! I'm familiar with the river currents, I know what they can do to a helpless boat. You could have been lost to us forever!"

"Now listen here, Cabe," John Ed said, barrelling toward them, "there's no reason to be talking like that. You're upsetting Dolly and she's upset enough already—and so's Laura."

"Yes, Laura's upset! Hasn't she had enough trouble without you jumping down her throat!" Pearl demanded from where she stood, detained, just barely, by Dolly's hand.

"I'm sorry, I didn't mean to jump down throats," Cabe intoned, inhaled, then burst out again, "But damn it, John Ed, you know it's a miracle that that boat isn't piled up on Frying Pan Shoals right this minute! Laura, I swear I could—"

"Daddy, don't holler at Laura!" Heather said indignantly. "It wasn't her fault we got lost, the boat ran out of gas."

"You ran out of gas?" Cabe asked incredulously, and Laura mentally groaned at the carelessness implicit in that. Setting Heather down, he straightened and leveled his gaze on her again.

Before he could speak, Heather jerked at his pant leg. "I *said*, don't holler at Laura, please. She rowed and rowed even though her hands were hurting and we went right past the big black rocks right into the beach—" She gulped air. "Just like she said we would. She's a brave hero, Daddy. I am, too. So you quit hollering at us!" Warily she glanced at Michele. "Hi."

Michele responded unsteadily, "Hi, darling." Kneeling, she clasped Heather's arms. "Do you know who I am?"

"Yes. You're Mommy," Heather said, wriggling free. Her grave little face broke into a smile. "This is my Miss Laura—and there's my kitty!"

She ran off, unable to take any more grown-up emotional displays, Laura suspected. Feeling a grubby, wind-blown mess, she returned Michele's gracious hello with a brief, intense scrutiny that made her heart sink. Cabe's wife—his ex-wife, she corrected herself—was appealingly lovely. Her immaculate attire, alligator pumps, an unstructured red jacket and fitted skirt, were tailor-made for her statuesque body. The graceful knot of golden hair wound atop her head lent her even more height. Delphinium blue eyes, outlined with kohl, were swimming with tears.

Ruefully, she asked Cabe for a handkerchief. Taking the one he handed her with a wry, knowing smile, she daubed delicately at teardrops.

Laura's eyes were blazingly dry. The intimacy of that smile had turned suspicion into certainty. She choked down a laugh at the terrible irony of it all. She had made her choice, only to find there was no choice to be made. Cabe still loved his wife—his *ex-wife*—oh, what did it matter! she thought wretchedly. In desperate need of help to conceal the pain knifing her heart, she buried her face in the shoulder of whichever aunt was hugging her breathless.

Her composure somewhat restored, she lifted her chin. "Cabe, Michele, I apologize for the distress I've inadvertently caused. Now if you'll excuse me—"

Cabe caught her arm. "Laura, wait a minute—"

Laura pulled away. She did not bother to look at him, and sounded merely irritable. "Cabe, I'm tired, achy, in desperate need of a long, hot bath. Now excuse me, please, I'm going home."

"And I'm going with her," Dolly informed him. "I'm sorry about abandoning Heather, but you'll have to find yourself a new housekeeper. Laura, honey, let me see those hands—look at this, will you just look at this!" she wheeled on Cabe again, displaying one of Laura's blistered palms and evoking an outraged gasp from Pearl. "Lord if she hasn't rowed the skin right off her hands getting Heather to safety—and you start taking her head off the instant she sets foot on the dock! Come on, Pearl, let's go take care of our mistreated girl!"

Glancing at Cabe's sharpening features, John Ed tried to get a moderating word in, but Dolly gave him a *look*. Fighting a hysterical urge to laugh and cry simultaneously, Laura walked on in a glassy-eyed daze.

Bathed and fed, however, she felt more responsive to the situation, and lost no time trying to change Dolly's mind about quitting her job. The best she could do was get a promise from her aunt to think about it.

Both aunts hovered like mother hens with one ailing chick. Both tippy-toed around Michele's startling appearance on the scene and that was annoying, too. When Laura brought it up, Dolly's eyes started to tear. "It's all my fault," she burst out. "I should have told you about how he acted when he got her letter. Then you'd have had some warning."

Laura rubbed her throbbing temples. "Aunt Dolly, I don't know what you think is your fault, but it isn't, so stop fretting yourself," she replied wearily. "Please, everyone just go on home now and let me get some rest."

Contrarily, when they did leave her alone, Laura felt an acute need for companionship. Stoically she resisted her impulse to call them back. But as dusk flowed into a sultry summer night, loneliness and despair overwhelmed her. Yielding to it, she dialed her aunts' number with shaking fingers.

"Mary Laura, are you all right?" Dolly asked sharply.

"Yes, I'm—" Laura's voice altered to a bleak mesa of pain. "No, I'm not. Aunt Dolly, can I come spend the night with you and be a child again, just for a little while?"

* * *

Laura was building a pyramid of canned peaches when Cabe came into the store the next morning. "Laura, can we talk?" he asked from behind her.

His quiet voice acted like a shout on her system. Turning, she clutched the shelf to steady herself. Their eyes met. Immediately she was caught up in a desperate battle between equally matched desire and conviction.

"Yes, of course," she replied, a little cool but cordial. "Where's Michele, with Heather?"

"Yes. That's one of the reasons I wanted to talk to you."

"Cabe, if you're working up to an apology for blowing your stack again, forget it. You had every right to be upset, you love that precious little girl."

"There were two precious girls involved in my upset." Cabe bit back the words hammering in his lips and compromised with a musing, "Funny, isn't it, how old clichés retain their truths? I didn't realize how precious until I thought I might lose you. Laura, you know I…" He spread his big hands, his smile dry as alum. "Well, suffice it to say you mean a lot to me."

Laura lowered her lashes. "I've never been in doubt of that, Cabe. You want to talk to me about Michele?"

"Yes. She'll be around for a day or two. I want Heather to decide for herself if she wants to know her mother. Then we'll see about visitation privileges." Unable to resist, Cabe ran a strand of silky brown hair through his fingers. He was dying to hold her. "This is all your doing, you know. You made me change my way of thinking."

"I'm glad, Cabe, glad for you all." Laura dug her nails into her palms to restrain the urge to tell him of her decision. It wasn't her nature to give up something she wanted without a fight. But her convictions were deep and strong. If there was the slightest chance that Heather might have both her parents again, then she had to bow out.

Blasted conscience! Laura thought with such gallant humor she made herself proud. "Good luck and—and let me know how it turns out," she said before hurrying up front to tend a customer. Her heart was breaking. Doggedly she told herself she'd done the right thing. She must remember that nobility had its own rewards.

Pearl came downstairs a few minutes later, charm bracelet tinkling. "Honey, was that Cabe I saw going out the gate?"

"Yes. He stopped by to tell me how Heather's doing," Laura replied just as lightly. Downplaying her heartache was taxing, but she couldn't bear any more worried looks. That evening she went home and threw herself on the bed to weep the desperately needed catharsis of tears.

The night was incredibly long, and the following day had enough hours in it to make a week. Laura thought it quite possible she might die from the rewards of being noble.

Rain forced her to drive the station wagon home from work and she sat in it for a startled moment, wondering why the cottage lights were on. Analyzing KK's faint bark, she relaxed. He was talking, not warning. A sensuous thrill replaced alarm as she hurried up the steps. She knew who was inside even before she opened the door.

"Cabe? What on earth are you—" She stopped dead. "What is this?"

"What? You don't recognize your grandmother's desk?"

"Yes, of course I do, but I—but you…" She flung up her hands. "Why?"

"Because I wanted to. Did you honestly think I would let you part with this just because you needed money?"

"It's not your place to decide…" Laura let it trail away and simply stared at him as she needed to do for the next hundred years or so. He wore his favorite outfit of knit shirt and faded jeans, and the leaping flame of desire burned brighter in her than ever. She didn't know what to say. So she stared at him.

Cabe watched her face, his heart in his mouth, pounding its urgent hope. The past two days absence from Laura and the loved ones she had so generously shared had led him to two stark discoveries.

One was that Mary Laura Richards was unforgettable.

The second was that he needed people.

But more than anything or anyone, he needed her. She had told him she loved him and he was hanging his entire stock of reviving dreams on that. Whether or not she loved him enough to accept his limitations he didn't know, but of one thing he was certain. He had to find out whatever the cost.

"Laura, I know you've been avoiding me, and I understand why. But I had to tell you this. I love you. In every way possible, I love you. You brought me alive again, made me clean and whole and happier than I ever thought possible."

He had to pause; his voice had become husky to the point of physical pain. She had grown very still. Her eyes, impossibly wide, were riveted on his face, her head was tilted as if she were listening to some distant music. Her lips curved. He cleared his throat. Again.

"I know there's a chance I can't give you that green-eyed ladykiller of a son you want so much, that I want so much— No, please, darling, let me finish," he said as her lovely mouth opened. "But there's also a chance I can. A slim one, I know that, but for you I'd take it—"

Fingers laid across his lips stopped him. "Oh, Cabe, that isn't why I've been avoiding you. That little mishap with the boat made me realize a few things, too. Namely that I can live without children, but I can't live without you. But I thought maybe you and Michele—"

"You thought what?" he growled.

"Well, you see, there's Heather. I love her, too, and I thought it would be best," she explained none too lucidly.

But Cabe understood, and it was another jolt of happiness to add to the strain on his manly dignity. "Yes, you would," he said. With exquisite delicacy, he gave his fingers the incomparable pleasure of relearning the shape of her face.

Quivering inside, afraid to move quickly least she break the tender moment, Laura slowly slid her hands over his.

She drew them down and turned them over. The weren't el
egant hands, or even particularly attractive. They wer
simply big, strong hands that could gentle to a lover's touch
or soothe a frightened child as easily as they could split a
hickory log with one mighty swing of the ax.

Or carry a woman to bed, she exulted as he laughed joy
ously and lifted her off the floor. So easily did he carry he
that her body was only faintly aware of his uneven gait

"Am I going to be marrying you anytime soon?" she asked
curiously.

"You just try getting out of it," he said, scowling fero
ciously.

"Huh." Laura threw back her head and laughed as a
wonderful thought formed in the glorious chaos of he
mind.

"What?" Cabe demanded, tumbling with her onto the
yielding bed.

"I was just thinking—what with Pearl and Dolly and your
family and my family and the Fair Harbor Ladies' Club
ours is bound to be the biggest, happiest, most uproariou
wedding in the history of Brunswick County!"

"Oh, my Lord," Cabe groaned at the picture she painted

"But Cabe, remember," Laura murmured, "After the
wedding, comes the honeymoon."

*   *   *   *   *

𝒟 Silhouette Desire

COMING NEXT MONTH

#379 MIDNIGHT RAMBLER—Linda Barlow
Headmistress Dany Holland had suspicions about Max Rambler.
Vampires belonged in storybooks, but when strange nocturnal events
threatened her students, she was determined to find out Max's secret.

#380 EAGLE'S PREY—Lucy Gordon
Photographing eagles had brought Sara to Farraway Island, but it
was Rorke Calvin who kept her there. His plans for revenge were
almost ripe—could she convince him to give them up for love?

#381 GIVE AND TAKE—Anna Schmidt
Set designer Marlo Fletcher was asked to dress the windows of
Carrington's department store. Sparks flew between her and
Josh Carrington—who would think that matters of the heart were
such a give-and-take business?

#382 NO LAUGHING MATTER—Marie Nicole
Writer Marti McGregor lived by her wit and spent a lot of time hiding
behind it. Producer Stephen Townsend was determined to break
through her defenses—for love was no laughing matter.

#383 CARNIVAL MADNESS—Erin Ross
Tired of nothing but parties, Elizabeth fled the latest Venetian
costume ball, only to find herself in the arms of a waiting gondolier.
Roberto was nothing that he seemed . . . but all that she desired.

#384 LOST AND FOUND—Robin Elliott
Kendra had no intention of getting involved with her neighbor *or* his
pet rabbit. But Joseph wasn't about to let this enchanting woman
misplace the love he'd searched a lifetime to find!

AVAILABLE NOW:

ATTRACTIVE, SPACE SAVING BOOK RACK

Display your most prized novels on this handsome and sturdy book rack. The hand-rubbed walnut finish will blend into your library decor with quiet elegance, providing a practical organizer for your favorite hard-or soft-covered books.

Only $9.95

Approximately 16" x 8" when assembled

Assembles in seconds!

To order, rush your name, address and zip code, along with a check or money order for $10.70* ($9.95 plus 75¢ postage and handling) payable to *Silhouette Books*.

Silhouette Books
Book Rack Offer
901 Fuhrmann Blvd.
P.O. Box 1396
Buffalo, NY 14269-1396

Offer not available in Canada.

BKR-2A

*New York and Iowa residents add appropriate sales tax.

Starting in October...

SHADOWS ON THE NILE

by

Heather Graham Pozzessere

A romantic short story in six installments from best-selling author Heather Graham Pozzessere.

The first chapter of this intriguing romance will appear in all Silhouette titles published in October. The remaining five chapters will appear, one per month, in Silhouette Intimate Moments' titles for November through March '88.

Don't miss "*Shadows on the Nile*"—a special treat, coming to you in October. Only from Silhouette Books.

Be There!

IMSS-1

Silhouette Desire

ANOTHER BRIDE FOR A BRANIGAN BROTHER!
Available September 1987
by
Leslie Davis Guccione

The cranberry-growing Branigan brothers are at it again! In #376 *Something in Common*, feisty Erin O'Connor teaches Kevin, the eldest of the six brothers, a much-needed lesson in love.

It all began in October 1986 with Drew Branigan's crusade to make Holly Bancroft see the error of her ways in #311 *Bittersweet Harvest*.

Then Drew's hoodlum-turned-cop younger brother, Ryan, gets his chance to win his childhood sweetheart in #353 *Still Waters*, published May 1987.

Don't miss out on any of the Branigan family fun, coming to you in the Silhouette Desire line.
